THE TOWER

THE TOWER

A novel by

Sheila McDermid

GWASG PANTYCELYN

Published with the financial support of the Arts Council of Wales
Cyhoeddwyd gyda chefnogaeth ariannol Cyngor Celfyddydau Cymru

ISBN 1 874786 99 2

Cover illustration: Ian Griffith

Printed in Wales
Argraffwyd yng Nghymru

ACKNOWLEDGEMENTS

I wish to thank: The Arts Council of Wales for their support; Simon Rees for his encouragement and advice; all at Gwasg Pantycelyn, in particular for the space they gave me – The Tower remained a 'work in progress' right up to publication; and my friends for being themselves.

Diolch and slàinte.

One

Difficult, still, not to think of it as Yugoslavia.

So long ago, so far away. That summer. The summer, perhaps, when I finally realised other people were as real as I was. __Am__ I mean.

I squeezed my eyes shut, then opened them again to the room around me. All I could see was the pale green duvet draped across the cot sides and the pinky-grey wall beyond the end of the bed. And on the wall the clock with the hands that seemed so reluctant to move.

I managed to roll my head slightly so I could look towards the window. Large irregular flakes of snow floated close to the pane, some falling against it slithering down melting. And beyond, the air was dense with white drifts and swirls so the shape of the wind was easier to see than the shapes of the variegated greys of the garden and the sky. The sounds of the slow-moving traffic were distant, muffled.

Trapped in a time out of time. And the walls closing in.

No.

Yugoslavia. And my mind fled again to that time. That summer. Turned up its colour, movement, warmth. Its certainty. As if it thought the past could animate the present. Compensate for it somehow.

Though, actually, it's the music of the time I remember most – and the energy of it.

There was 'Ruby Tuesday' by the Stones, and the locals' version, 'Rube Utorake' – somehow they managed to make it sound so melancholy. We danced on the terraces till the exuberance of the waking birds defeated the band and we had just one more drink watching the dawn ignite the sky, the sea.

Timeless.

Unchanging.

'Hey Jude', Sacha Distel. Young men diving from the high rocks, making sure we were watching. And the cicadas, and the heat, and the clear brightness of the light.

Thunderstorms.

Skinny-dipping in the Adriatic by moonlight, the water still warm. The glow of the embers of the driftwood fires we'd built on the beach's sharp grey pebbles. Drift-smoke. Strong cheese and heavy, char-warmed bread.

The night-smell of the Mimosas.

Smoke – acrid, chest-tightening, re-awakening the churning, fluttering inside.

Mimosas. The night-smell of the Mimosas.

Then there was that morning at the end of summer.

Concentrate, Kate. Visualise it.

I'd gone on the ferry. The scruffy local ferry, crossing the Gulf from Pula to the markets in Venice. I'd arrived at the last moment, and the boat was already too full, as the local boats always were.

◆

I leapt down onto the deck, hair and fringed shoulder-bag flying, just as they cast off. I grabbed the rail as the boat rocked and juddered and the engine spurted smudges of oil-laden smoke . . .

Smoke.

Spurted smudges of oil-laden smoke into the hot blue of the sky. I hardly had time to catch my breath and grin back at the boy coiling the rope before we started to chug from the dock. Nice eyes he had – but a boy just.

I looked for a better place, then tottered across the deck towards it between all the people and their strewn belongings. There were dishevel-bearded goats bleating, straining at the hairy string wound around the fists of unshaven men who smelled much as they did. There were huddles of black-shrouded women hugging to their knees lidded baskets jumping with the flutterings and squawkings of claustrophobic hens. One put her hand up to steady me as I squeezed past her. From a radio aft a local group wailed 'Rube

Utorake' in a minor key. There were wicker baskets over-filled with nectarines and courgettes and carvings in two-tone wood.

I joined too many people clinging to the wet pole in the centre of the deck – they adjusted their hands to make a space at my height. We sailed from the harbour straight into the wind, swaying, bumping into each other. I lifted my face and my hair streamed out behind me, my skin tightening to the cold and the wildness of the sea and the sky. We clung, as far as we could get from the icy needles of foam scooped up to the wind by our dipping bow. But they still stung and drenched us. I tasted the salt on my lips.

The boat started to yaw and creak and the press of people eased as more and more of them made trips to the side. You wouldn't have thought that the women would have been allowed to vomit in public.

Soon it seemed as if it was only myself and the man next to me who weren't sick. He was standing into the wind too, swaying with the energy of it. He was tall and heavy with a soft beard, brown, fading round the edges, and hair to his shoulders. He was middle-aged, except in the light of his eyes.

He grinned at me and I looked away, then, "Are you old enough to drink šljivovica?" he asked in bad German.

I told him the truth, in German, not knowing what other languages to try, but speaking slowly and loudly so that he could understand – still he handed me his flask. Metal it was, maybe silver, and cold. His hands were strong-looking, but rough – they didn't seem to go with the rest of him somehow. The brandy burnt the back of my throat.

I handed him back the flask and the boat lurched us together. The damp salt-stiffness of his denims felt rough even against the goose-pimpled numbness of my thighs, and I wished I'd worn a longer skirt.

"Are we changing course?" I asked, as I tried to back away up the tilt of the deck from him. The wind and waves were attacking us from a different direction.

"Yes," he said, "we're heading up the peninsula towards Trieste. Clever of you to notice." He managed to get the flask back into his pocket, and took a step to the side. "You are used to the sea?"

"Yes," I told him, "I come from a small island."

"Ah," he said, "I come from Heidelberg, to get further from the sea is difficult."

"Oh, but isn't that in Germany?"

"Yes." He paused. "Do I not speak your standard British German?"

I looked up and saw that his eyes were laughing. But not at me. Probably.

"My name is Hartmutt," he said. We risked letting go of the pole for long enough to shake hands. Somehow his was still warm. He suggested we speak in English and I agreed, being careful to explain that it wasn't my first language either. I didn't know why he was wearing after-shave when he had a beard. It was something with sandalwood in it.

The sea got rougher. We could see the head of the captain in his little hutch. Some of the men went to speak to him but he just waved his arms and got angrier, and drank more, and spoke on the radio. We could hear the static.

Then, to starboard, fleetingly, as we rose with the swell, we saw the shore, but didn't turn towards it. We seemed to be hugging the coast round to Venice, though the weather wasn't that bad.

Then Hartmutt pointed back out into the bay. I screwed up my eyes and eventually I saw, in a wave as it hollowed, a grey tube shape pointing upwards, the suggestion of a grey shape under it. Then I saw more. Maybe a dozen or more.

"What are they?" I asked, knowing, but not wanting, the answer.

"Mmm, is submarines the word?"

"Yes," I said, hearing my voice rise, "but the tube things – what are the tube things called?"

He put his hand, warm, on my shoulder. "I don't know, my dear," he said, then grabbed for the pole again as a wave crashed into our side, "didn't you need the English word for the seeing tubes of the under-water boats on your island either?"

"No," I said, "in any language we just needed the words for midges and sheep. Oh, and for ferry departure timetables." I caught his smile as I turned away, sudden tears stinging my eyes.

In the end we agreed they were called hydroscopes, though we both knew it was the wrong word. You could feel the fear on the boat, even the animals were quiet.

He looked round. "You must be the only person on the boat who hasn't lived through a war," he said.

My mouth went dry and I got a picture in my mind of the huge grey Russian ships that had been piling into the harbour in the last week or so, huddled tight so some of them couldn't get near the shore. If only they had spread out they would all have been able to get near the shore. I was suddenly very aware of the differences in the movements of the boat and the horizon and my stomach. He passed me his flask and I drank and looked only at the horizon, and the feeling went. Cold the flask was. Smooth.

Then we turned back out into the Bay and soon there was only the sea and the sky and the ache of arms clinging against the bucking of the boat. We couldn't hear ourselves speak above the roaring of the wind and the waves, the crashes and judders of our boat.

When first we saw land it was difficult to believe it was real, though there were seagulls in plenty wheeling and crying to tell us it was so.

When we hove to the boat was low in the water below the jetty and they had to prop a wide plank from the side to the shore at too steep a slope. We all had to be hauled and pushed up it. I learnt some new words from the goat-owners. And when we got to dry land – though it was raining by then – Hartmutt and I just stood in the mêlée for a while. It seemed rude, somehow, just to say goodbye.

He saw me looking at my watch.

"It's alright," he said, "it's a different time-zone, we must change the time we have back an hour."

I'd still be well over half an hour later than I'd told her to expect me.

"I'm going for a hot drink to warm myself up – and our safe arrival seems to need a celebration," he said. "Will you join me?"

"Yes," I said.

So we went to St Mark's square for a coffee. Espresso, though we'd asked for cappuccino – we hadn't the heart to tell the waiter, he looked scared. The few tourists there were in the square looked as if they were there by accident, and didn't want to be. The drying rat-tails of my hair clung to my cheeks. The coffee smell was strong, with the dog-like undertones of our dampness. We just sat for a while, he seemed as uncertain as I was.

"You are still at school? Yes?" he asked eventually.

"Not for much longer," I said, "I'm going to Edinburgh. I'm going to be a linguist."

"Ahh," he said, grinning into his coffee cup.

The grey flagstones of the square looked dull, and the white line patterns of the paler flags all seemed to lead to tight bunches of soldiers in khaki with khaki berets and brown shoes, brown belts. I didn't know what country they came from. The raining sky and the khaki seemed to have drained all the colour from the mosaics. There were hardly any pigeons. The coffee was too strong and left a bitterness in my mouth.

"Why don't you write to me in German?" he asked, "it might help you. Or English – you say that's not your first language either."

"I wonder, sometimes, if words are."

He laughed, then he smiled at me. We exchanged addresses, then he said he must go. He'd written 'girl on boat to conference' beside my name.

"I will walk with you to the house of your mother?"

"No, it's okay, thanks," I said, "it's not far."

I thought he was going to argue, but he didn't. Perhaps he meets girls on boats all the time. We stood and shook hands. He started off in one direction, so I went in another. At the corner I turned and waved at his back. He didn't turn.

The streets were like canyons, and the uneven pavements were beginning to steam as the sun came out. I wonder what he has to confer about.

Two

I went around another corner just to make sure he wouldn't see me. I looked at my watch. I'd be nearly two hours late, she'd be frantic. I got her letter out of my bag to check the address again. I tried to make sense of the map but, of course, she'd started it tracing my route from the jetty and I didn't know now where that was.

The writing was much more spidery and scrawled than usual. And the ink green. Green. I felt myself going hot again as I remembered its arrival at school. I suppose she imagined it was artistic.

The canal was narrow, and the washing strung across it was flapping, splattering water. However did they manage to peg it all on?

'Come on,' I told myself, 'you've got to get there.' I asked one or two people, showed them the map, and in the end managed to find a cafe that she'd marked on it. My drying shoes were tightening on my feet. The drainy smell of the place seemed to be seeping into me. So many arches and bridges there were.

Then I saw a building that looked like the one she'd described. I peered at my map again to be sure.

I pulled and pulled at the bell, there was no sound, difficult to be sure it was working. I stepped back and looked up at the windows, but I didn't know which one it was, and they were mostly shuttered. I could feel the churning of my stomach. The sea crossing it would be, and my being so late for my dinner.

Then, at last, I heard the soft padding of feet on the stair, they'd be able to tell me it was the wrong place. Then the door opened. The stair started from straight behind the door like the worst of the tenements in Glasgow. Smells of garlic and turpentine. Mum stood on the bottom step so it was as if I hadn't grown taller than her. She'd varnished her nails.

"Roberto, it's her," she yelled over her shoulder. There was a blur of words in a quick rural Italian I couldn't quite catch.

"The boat was late."

She looked at her wrist, but she wasn't wearing her watch. "Come away in," she said.

She had a cigarette in her hand so I couldn't hug her.

I followed her up the stair, her heels were naked and pink.

Roberto's room was at the top. A garret no less. He looked at me and continued tucking his vest into his jeans. I suppose he thought I'd never seen a hairy chest before.

It was a room of windows. The shutters were open and the light streamed in. Canvases were stacked against what walls there were with the only care that had been taken in the room. Two easels. Their canvases were facing one another. I couldn't see what was on them.

He stepped towards me hand outstretched. "Ciao," he said.

"Good afternoon," I said. I tried to pull my hand away, but he wouldn't let it go until he'd shaken it.

"There were submarines in the bay, we had to stay round by the coast."

"Come," he said, "you sit." I sat on a too soft chair and looked at my mother.

"How long till you go back to school now?" she asked.

"A fortnight," I said.

"You look well," she said.

"You'll be telling me next that I've grown." Her toe nails were painted too.

Roberto came over to me precariously carrying three glasses and a bottle of red wine. Mother lifted her hand as if to protest, then changed her mind. She perched on the arm of the chair opposite me whilst I accepted the glass of wine. He gave her a glass and was about to sit in the chair beside her, then sat on the floor to the side about halfway between us.

"This is cosy," I said.

She had to translate that for him.

"You live at a school in England?" Roberto asked.

"Scotland," I said.

My mother ground out her cigarette in a saucer. "Why don't you come and help me with some food?"

I looked around for a door to the kitchen. There was a curtain half pulled round one corner. Behind it I could see a lumpily made bed.

Then, on the floor next to one of the easels, I saw three sunflowers in her blue Chinese vase. She was still doing her flower paintings. I went over to the easel, I glanced at her, and she nodded. That painting was obviously his. I turned to the other easel. But that was her face, her face looking soft and sleepy. And her shoulders bare.

"But I liked your flower paintings, they were nice."

"Nice is about right."

"But Mum, you've always done flower paintings. They were good. Some of them were almost like photographs."

I looked again at her painting. It was sort of swervey and swirly – looked as if it'd been painted fast. It seemed to stand off the canvas, like a Catherine wheel sparking light. It made me feel something I didn't want to feel.

"I'm hungry if you're not," she said, "come and help me with some food. Roberto?"

"I will go out and buy some wine," he said.

He pulled on a jumper he picked from the pile on the back of the chair and we listened to his feet as they clattered downwards to the street.

I could feel the warmth of the sun as it beat strongly on the sky-light. I looked up. Illuminated bird-droppings. Already framed.

We heard the door slam, then she seemed to give herself a little shake. I followed her through a jangling bead curtain into the kitchen.

Just because they're staying in the same room it doesn't mean they're sleeping together.

The kitchen was small and cluttered, but they had found enough room, under the sink, for a rack full of wine.

She put on a pan of water to heat.

15

"How's your father?" she asked, bending and reaching a hand into the vegetable rack.

I could see the top of her head, her hair had some gray in it. She was the one who'd left.

"Something's happening," I said, "the Embassy's phoning all the time, but he says we'll not go back to Zagreb unless we have to."

She walked round me and picked up a jar of pasta. She was wearing the perfume she always wore. Coty L'Aimant. He used to buy it for her every Christmas.

"What do you call those things that stick up out of submarines so they can see things?" I asked.

"Periscopes." She threw the pasta into the water. It wasn't quite boiling.

"How is he?"

'Lonely,' I was going to say, but I turned and looked at her, and my eyes started to fill with tears too.

She gave me some onions to chop.

Three

Poor Mum, but how could I have understood then? Can we ever completely?

And with that thought I watched the past images fade – saw them replaced again by those of the present. The once pink walls, the end of the bed. I'd thought my mother so selfish all those years ago – I don't know what I'd expected her to do. Now I just remember her, then, as so vibrant and colourful – so alive.

I sighed and squinted at the clock face, the hands didn't seem to have moved. I listened. It was still ticking. Still, it'd stopped me thinking of the smoke.

I tried to visualise the face of my mother as it is now. But I couldn't see it. I told myself, 'white hair, the skin she insists on calling crumpled'. And again I saw her face as it'd been as she opened the door of the studio to me that day.

It's funny the way we are now, I suppose, my mother – her body just walking, walking, and her mind flowing free, unable to get the words out that match what's inside. Loose connections, but flowing light and free. And I lie here, barely able to move, and my mind returning, returning; to scenes, to places, to times, to people – trying to join it all up. Trying not to fall down the cracks.

The last time I saw her – how long has it been? I managed to move my head slightly on the pillow. The clouds were lighter and the snow had stopped, but the spattered opacity of the window made the garden seem even more bleak as it sank into the night. The first few leaves, uncurling from bud, clung, strangely mis-shapen, to the boughs. Daffodils cowered, half beaten to the sodden white-pocked soil. It was only the mist, swirling around the statue of Queen Victoria, that was missing. Why on earth don't they come and close the curtains? I'll be hearing the wails of the Ban-shee next.

The snow had been lying a sun-glinting purity when last I saw her. He'd put the chains on the car, and had driven slowly – leaning forward. I'd thought of a mole. And I'd sat, huddled in my blankets, amazed that they'd let me out, that the world was so vast and bright, the air so clean and fresh. Cold. A couple of weeks it must be just.

Alasdair and I'd quarrelled then too. She hadn't seemed to notice. She was speaking only Gàidhlig. The words of her childhood and youth. And mine. Before we'd left home.

How angry I'd been with him then, though I'd frozen it into the safety of silence, as he'd bent over me and we glared at each other, and she wandered around us glazed-eyed singing 'Chì Mi na Mòr-bheanna' – I see the mountains.

He'd wanted to send her back home where at least, he'd said, she'd be understood. Only he could have failed to realise that she didn't want to be understood, didn't want to understand.

I remembered my anger at the anxiety on the flushed face of him. The woody smell of his aftershave. The solidity of his body, his mind.

There's something they're not telling me. All of them.

"Mrs err . . . just let me tidy you up a bit." It was the youngest one, in too much of a hurry as usual, tweaking the downie from its snugness.

"Your husband's just having a word with the doctor, he'll be here in a minute."

"In that case, perhaps you'd better mess me up a bit more."

She closed my book and put it on the table, laying the book-mark neatly on the top of it.

"I see you don't think that's possible."

"He's got chrysanthemums."

She bustled out, leaving me to wait, watching, as the fire door slow- motioned towards its frame before thudding shut. The reverberations had hardly settled before the door was thrust open again and Hartmutt was moving towards me. He half-turned, pausing, caught the door and quietly pushed it to. I don't know why I was surprised it was Hartmutt. Or relieved. We certainly – but we aren't married, are we?

"Hallo, my dear, how are you today?" he bent to kiss me, laying the flowers down around my ankles somewhere.

"I was just thinking; do you remember the time we first met? On the boat, crossing to Venice?"

"Indeed." He pulled the only chair closer to the bed and sat on it. "You were wearing rather affecting pale blue knickers." He smiled, remembering, and we lapsed into a silence. He seemed tired.

"Sorry, my dear."

"Oh, Hartmutt, don't apologise. You don't know how good it is to have someone here, but not badgering me with questions."

"Yes, they do say you're less than forthcoming at present."

"Well, perhaps so, but I'm getting very good at listening. In fact, I've been wondering, whenever, if ever, I get out of this place if I shouldn't take up counselling. It's an expanding field, to be sure."

He creakingly tried to settle more comfortably on the too small chair.

"When was it, do you remember?" I asked.

The young nurse burst in again slopping water from a cut-glass vase.

"Shall I put your chrysanthemums in this for you, Dr Schilling?" she asked, setting it on my bedside table.

"Please," he said, "if you will."

I thought they were supposed to be mine.

We both watched while she hacked at the flowers' stems with ineffectual scissors and arranged them lankily in the vase. A rich rust colour they were with a soft arch to the petals of them.

"When was it?" I asked again as the door made to close behind her.

"When we met? Late sixties wasn't it? I was on my way to give my first paper, at a major conference, as first author. 1968. It seemed important then. Damned if I can remember the title of the thing. The Dalmatian excavation."

"'Not a stone unturned'?"

"I've been asking them if they think you'll be well enough to come out for a few days over Easter, it's a long way off yet – but something to aim at. If you want to."

"Yes." '. . . come out' – come home? "How old were you then?"

"When?"

"68."

"God, I don't know. Twenty six or seven."

"Funny, you know, I'd thought you middle aged then. Though I'm not that myself even now."

"Just if you want to. You don't have to decide yet. Also we'll have to wait and see how you are." He stood up.

"You're not going already, are you?" I asked, surprised how much I wanted him to stay. Wanted him to want to.

"You're not the easiest of people to visit at the moment, my dear. You always seem to want to be in another time, another place."

I heard the utter weariness in his voice and for the first time I really looked at him. He gathered me in his arms then, forgetting to lift with the pillow underneath, and my head flopped back. He moved his arm higher, hugged me to him.

"I don't know how to help you," he said, his voice thickening and muffled by my hair.

Face pressed against his thick jumper, held too tight, I struggled for breath. After what seemed a long time he laid me down gently on the pillows again.

"I will go, if you don't mind. You're tired too. I'll stay for longer tomorrow."

"I'll look in my diary to see if I'm free."

He bent to kiss me again. "The time will come again, my dear, the time will come."

The room seemed small when he'd gone, and I wished that I'd made more of an effort. The present didn't seem to be quite real. Or I didn't. I turned to look out of the window, but all I could see was the room reflected again in the blackness of the night beyond. I could see myself lying there, and the expression on my face. I squinted to try to see more clearly, to try to work out what it was an expression of. But I couldn't.

So tired. But tomorrow I'll try more. Again.

I tried to reach for my book, but she'd put it too far away. The next event will be the supper drink.

I turned to look at my chrysanthemums, the only things around, they were, with any colour and warmth to them. Though there was something wrong with them that I couldn't just place. I never even thanked him for them. Chrysanthemums? Can you get them at this time of year?

The young nurse came in again. "No rest for the wicked."

"What do you want me to do now?"

"I just want to give you a quick wash, make you more comfortable before we bring round the drinks, before I go off."

I made the effort to focus on her. "Going out are you?" I asked.

She looked a little surprised, glanced away, then back and our eyes met momentarily, "staying in, I hope," she said.

She can't be much older than . . . than?

Quite pretty, I suppose. She retrieved the bowl from the cupboard under the sink and began to fill it.

"What's his name then?" What's hers? She must have told me.

"Paul."

She prattled on about him all the time she was washing me, wetting my sheets – which made it easier.

"Nurse," I said, as she rearranged the things on my bedside table once more, "isn't it too early for chrysanthemums?"

"Well, it is here. Didn't you know? He came straight from the airport. Jersey or Holland or somewhere," she peeled off her disposable gloves and waved them vaguely before throwing them in the bin. "Very romantic." She tucked some of the hair unravelling from her plait down her collar. "Sorry for calling him your husband, by the way, I get a bit confused sometimes."

"The blind leading the blind is it?"

"Oh, I'm sure you've seen a lot more than I have. Oh, I should have said, he's coming to see you in the morning, on his way to work."

"Hartmutt?"

"No, the other one. I bet you're glad he doesn't work in this hospital."

The door opened slightly to reveal the navy blue-clad shoulder and sleek dark head of Sister Wilson. "Ahh, there you are, Jane," she said, "haven't you finished Mrs MacKinnon yet?"

"Oh sorry, Sister, just coming." She tore off her disposable apron and threw it after her gloves. She grinned at me, "I'll be back in a minute with the drinks."

The Sister came fully into the room. She straightened my duvet, and took my pulse. "You seem brighter this evening, love," she smiled, "and there's good news too. Dr Butler is back, she'll see you in the morning."

"What, the woman you told me about this afternoon?"

"Yes, Virginia Butler, you should get nurse to write down people's names for you – it might help you remember. You're very lucky, she's a busy lady, she doesn't take such an interest in everyone."

She straightened my duvet again, laid her hand for a moment on my shoulder, then went out.

'"Mrs MacKinnon."' I thought Alasdair and I were divorced. Maybe we are, and I haven't changed my name back. But Hartmutt, I remember now, he said he was going to give a talk somewhere, on something. No wonder he was tired. He must have carried them with him all the way in the plane, and I never even acknowledged them. He thinks chrysanthemums are my favourite.

I turned to the window, but someone had drawn the curtains. I closed my eyes, and for once the inside of them was just black.

✦

"Horlicks, Ovaltine, or tea?"

"Pardon?"

"Horlicks or tea? Been snoozing have you? Come on now, let me get you settled down."

For once she seemed in a hurry to leave me.

"Oh yes, Paul. Tell me about it in the morning, Jane."

"Wow," she beamed, "fancy you remembering, wait till I tell Sister."

I lay, waiting for sleep to come. I hummed 'Ruby Tuesday' to myself to keep my mind quiet. I couldn't remember the words.

Four

"Some things are better not known."

A startled silence lengthened between us.

"So," he said at last, "there it is. You finally admit it."

I was lying too flat to see all of his face and found myself watching, mesmerised, as the isolated movements of his lower teeth and lip, and his tongue writhing in the damp pinkness of his mouth seemed to mangle the sense out of the words.

I closed my eyes and concentrated on making my breathing deep and even, and after a moment I managed to ask, "admit what?"

"You know fine what," he said, his voice deepening, "you know more than you're saying."

"Alasdair, I'm not doing it on purpose." I looked at him again. "I really don't know what's happened. Only parts of it anyway."

He leant over me, so his whole face came glaringly into view.

"Your body'll heal, mostly, eventually, they say, but how can your mind if you won't face up to what's happened? How can mine if you won't tell me?"

In the distance the tea trolley rattled, and canned laughter issued inanely from a television.

"Your mother's making the same choice. The easy way out. But you haven't the right to make that choice for me. You must know what happened to Sarah. You must."

"Sarah? Who's Sarah?"

Something was happening to my chest, I couldn't get the air to go into it. I couldn't breathe. There was a roaring, a ringing in my ears.

"Och, not again," I heard his voice as if from a great distance, "I'm getting sick of this."

He put his arm crooked under my shoulders and head, lifted me, re-arranged the pillows, and propped me up on them. He stayed leaning over me while my breathing eased and the ringing in my ears quietened.

"Sorry," he said, "sorry. They keep telling me not to ask about her. The only thing I need to know."

He stood for a moment looking around, looking anywhere but at me.

"I'd better go. This isn't doing either of us any good."

The door opened and a nurse wheeled the trolley half in, jamming the door open with it.

"Oh, Dr MacKinnon, good. Do you mind giving this to her for me?"

"Not at all," he said, taking the cup of tea from her.

She clattered on down the corridor leaving the released door to thud back into place.

He lifted me up again and gave me my tea quickly, efficiently, in silence. He stood and put the cup down on my bedside table.

"I really will be going now," he said.

"Back to your other corpses, is it?" I asked.

"No," he said, "I'm not going to the lab. I'll see you again."

"Yes," I said. 'Perhaps,' I told myself. 'I can tell them I'll not see him again.' But, somehow, I knew I mustn't do that, though my mind seemed to bounce off knowing just why.

He paused and turned in the doorway as if to say something. But he thought the better of it.

Choice. I lay and looked at the dingy pastel pink of the ceiling and the top of the wall opposite me. How can anyone possibly imagine I choose to be like this?

After a moment I sighed and looked for my book. I managed to manoeuvre it from the table and prop it up, open. The page was at the wrong angle for me to read it, but they wouldn't know that if they looked at me through the window in the door. And, if the luck was with me, they'd just let me be.

✦

Jane came in with my lunch tray. How can you ever be hungry if all you ever do is lie and not move? She put the tray down on the table and wedged another pillow under my head. She sat down on the chair beside the bed and, without asking me if I wanted it, began to shovel the mush in. After a moment she leapt up and, too late, put a towel round my neck instead of the forgotten bib.

I remember a nurse who'd been in our crowd when Alasdair and I were students. She'd said that when they were training they were made to run up a stair of four flights before feeding each other with dry cornflakes so they'd know what it was like, and remember, when they were let loose on patients. But the Trusts can only afford heart-lung transplants and intra-uterine operations now, not boring ordinarily-sick people and un-warranted cornflakes.

"You look how I feel."

"Pardon?"

"I was saying, Mrs MacKinnon, that you don't look too happy this morning."

"Oh, I'm alright, just a little tired, though I can't imagine why."

"You're getting better. That's something."

She rubbed some of the larger lumps against the side of the bowl with the back of the spoon and we both watched them disintegrate. The mush was thick and gloopy green but there was something strangely hunger-inducing about the smell of it. The body has a mind of its own.

"What made you decide to be a nurse, Jane?"

She sighed, "I wonder, sometimes, if it's the right thing."

I tried to focus on her face, the skin of it looked so fresh and smooth. "You try very hard," I told her.

Our eyes met for a moment and I tried to think of something more positive to say. But she spoke before I came up with anything.

"What did you use to be again?" she asked.

"A linguist."

"Oh yes that's right, and, oh sorry . . ." looking confused she shoved another spoonful into my mouth.

Something else she'd been told to keep from me.

"Well, tell me about your evening then," I said, "if you want to." Poor girl, it's not her fault. "How did it go?"

She put the bowl down and was just about to tell me when her pager went off. She took it out of her pocket, looked at it, and sighed.

"They need me on the main ward," she said, "I'll be back as soon as I can."

I managed to move my head slightly on the pillow, and looked out of the window. The sun was actually out, obscured only by a mist which it was trying to thin with its warmth.

'. . . our crowd when Alasdair and I were students'. It doesn't seem possible now that I was in love with him then. The first time I really was with anyone. Difficult to remember it untainted with what's happened since. Though I suppose that's how all memory is – at best.

Jane came in again and sat herself down beside me. "Sorry, about that," she said, "one of the old ladies fell out of bed – she's okay, but it took three of us to get her back in."

She picked up the bowl and started to feed me again. Cold the purée was now too.

"You were going to tell me about your evening with Paul. How it went," I said.

"Oh, that. Yes. Okay." She looked towards the window.

"You don't sound very enthusiastic."

She put the bowl down, and sighed again, "We had a takeaway and watched the telly."

"Oh, but I thought . . ."

"I got my period didn't I?"

"Oh dear."

She gave me a mouthful of the luke-warm tea. Someone had forgotten again that I don't take sugar. "You don't know how lucky you are being finished with all that."

"Finished with all what?"

"Well, er," she glanced at me uncomfortably, "I suppose you've only been here for five or six weeks. Maybe it's the shock."

"How old do you think I am?"

She picked up the chart from the end of the bed and looked at it. "Oh, sorry. That's not very old. Must be the shock."

"What shock?"

"I don't know, of whatever happened." She picked up the tray.

"How do you know it was a shock if you don't know what happened?" I could hear myself starting to shout. "Why won't any of you tell me?"

Jane backed towards the door.

"How can any of you imagine I don't want to remember?"

"I'd better go," she said without looking at me, "Sister'll be wondering where I've got to." She fled.

She'd taken the tea, and I'd not drunk it.

Five

"Hallo, love."

I tried to turn at the sound of Hartmutt's voice. But I was flat on my back and I couldn't.

"Sorry," he said, appearing at the side I could turn my head to and see him properly, "sorry, love." He bent to kiss me. "And how are you today?"

"Oh Hartmutt," I said, "I'm so sorry. The chrysanthemums. They're so beautiful, and you must have been so tired. I never even thanked you for them."

He smiled, "It's alright, don't worry. I saw your eyes keep going to them. A few weeks ago you didn't even recognise me. I'm not complaining now." He sat down in his chair. He was wearing shoes, it must be the weekend.

"I seem to be getting so grouchy, it's awful."

"Alasdair phoned," he said, "asked me to tell you he's sorry." He crossed his legs and leant back.

"Alasdair phoned you?"

"Yes, my dear. Any moment now we'll all have to apologise for apologising so much," he smiled at me, relaxing.

"He said he'd been awake most of the night and shouldn't really have come in to see you this morning. He wants to come again tomorrow evening if you'll have him."

"Hartmutt, who's Sarah?"

He bent and clicked open the catch on his briefcase. He showed me the book I'd asked him to bring in, then put it on my bedside table. The bend had raised his colour.

"Did Alasdair's visit upset you? He is under quite a strain too, you know."

"Oh, I suppose he did a bit, him and that stupid woman. But

28

'Hartmutt, I want to know who Sarah is."

He straightened my duvet, brushed back some hair that was falling across my eye. "Tell me about the stupid woman first."

I sighed, did he really think I'd be put off so easily?

"Hartmutt," I asked, "have you registered with a doctor here for your blood pressure tablets?"

"Oh, I just got Alasdair to give me a prescription the other night. Time enough to sort things like that out when we all know what we're doing."

He closed his brief case and put it under his chair. "The woman," he said.

"Oh it's just that psychiatrist I'm meaning," I said, "Virginia – I know what pigeonhole I'm going to squeeze you into – Butler."

He grinned. "Poor woman, did you give her a hard time?"

"Hartmutt," I said, "I thought you were supposed to be on my side."

"You feel there are sides in this?"

I looked up and found his eyes watching me. His lovely familiar dark blue flecked eyes. With a sadness in them I wasn't used to seeing there.

"I don't know," I said, "I really don't know. It can hardly be anything good – whatever happened – can it? To have left me like this."

"The imagination is a terrible thing." He closed his eyes for a moment, "we'll all be better when we know."

"Yes, but she said to trust my mind, that it knows what it's doing. And what my mind has decided is not to know."

"For the moment, yes." He straightened his legs. "But every time I see you now you're better than the last. Nearly every time."

"I don't see where my mother fits in. Was she with me?"

"Yes, she was with you."

I waited for him to go on – but he didn't.

"Oh, to be fair, perhaps I just expected too much from her. Virginia. She got such a big build up." I got a picture in my mind of her tight- lipped face at the end of our interview.

"Oh, Hartmutt," I said, "if she's the best there is – we may as well give up now."

But he just laughed and picked up my hand. "You're bound to feel a bit threatened by her, when you're so uncertain. It's bound to take a little time."

I saw him raise my hand to his lips and kiss it.

He said, "She was pleased with how it went."

"You're all talking about me behind my back. You're all keeping things from me." I was surprised at the anger I heard in my voice. The anger I felt.

"I'm sorry," he said, "but we're doing our best not to rush you. To risk sending you back to the way you were. It's not always easy." He got up and walked over to the window.

And suddenly I could hear again her smoke-hoarse voice.

✦

"There are intriguing associations," she said, "between what your mind's choosing to dwell on and your current situation. Trust your mind, on some level it knows what it's doing, what it needs."

Her eyes had seemed to look at me without seeing. Pale eyes.

"Try to look at it in that light, it'll give you the necessary distance, perspective, make it more manageable."

✦

The way I am now. How can I even speak to someone who thinks of it as intriguing? And I don't need her to dissect and categorize my life, I just need to recall the missing week – however long it is.

✦

She smiled. "We need to know more. We need to understand the inter-relatedness of all these disparate memories. What their meaning is for you."

✦

"Speak for yourself," I should have said, "what I need is a bottle of wine and a helicopter." I should have told her I wasn't going to see her again.

I looked past Hartmutt out of the window, but it was snowing again and all I could see were the wind-driven slashes of snow, and the lowering greyness of the sky. Stupid woman she is, they're just random memories – I've got to think of something while I'm lying here. Entertain myself.

The door opened and Hartmutt turned.

"Oh sorry, Dr Schilling, I'll come back later." It was Jane.

"No, no, it's alright," he said, starting across the room. He seemed relieved to see her. "I could do with a coffee. You do whatever you have to do, then I'll come back."

"Okay thanks," said Jane, "I just have to take her temp. and things. It'll not take more than a couple of minutes."

"She means she'll pretend to stick pins into my body to try to convince me I can't feel it."

I could see the things in her hand. Why do they have to do it every single bloody day? Remind me again and again of my agonising numbness – and the threat of it leaving me.

I looked to Hartmutt, "A voodoo doll," I said, "that's all I am now."

But he just smiled at me, and left.

◆

I could hear him, outside the closed door, talking to Jane in a subdued voice. He must have been waiting for her to leave. There was someone else there too. Eventually he came in and came round the bed and kissed me again.

"Hartmutt, who's Sarah?"

He sighed and sat down. He was quiet for a moment, then he picked up my hand. I watched him stroke it. Then he just held it. I could see my fingers turning white.

Quietly he said, "Sarah is Alasdair's daughter." He leaned closer towards me. "And yours."

"Don't be ridiculous," I said. His face seemed to blur and recede, though his body stayed just the same.

Slowly, as if talking to an idiot, he said, "Sarah is your daughter."

"I wouldn't have forgotten that."

"It seems you have."

There was a silence. His face returned to normal, but everything seemed sort of distant somehow.

"But I've only forgotten a few weeks," I said, "have some other things a bit confused," I looked at my hand, he was still holding it. "You don't mean – she can't be just a few weeks old."

"No, no."

"Well, how old is she then?"

"I'm not exactly sure, to tell you the truth."

"Now I'm beginning to believe you."

"No love, she does exist. I've met her quite a few times over the years. A lovely girl."

He looked out of the window, frowning, for a moment, then back at me.

"I suppose she must be about the age you were when we first met."

There was a long silence.

I tried to think of something to say, something to think, but my mind was blank. I looked to him but he was watching me, waiting. I looked away.

Eventually he looked at his watch, and retrieved his briefcase.

"You're seeing Dr Butler again in the morning?" he asked.

"Yes," I said. My voice sounded hoarse. "I'll have to remember not to tell her where I come from."

"Why?" He stood up.

"Small Scottish island. She'll put me down for Satanic abuse."

"Isn't that social workers?" I could hear him trying to force a lighter note into his voice.

"Same difference," I said. "People who won't let you be."

After he'd gone I tried to visualise 'Sarah', but the whole idea was just unimaginable. After a while I just let my mind drift back as it wanted, so much, to do. It went again to the same time, the same place.

✦

"No," Dad said, "I don't think it would have been better if you'd gone to Eilean a' Gaoth to stay with your Nan for the school holiday. I'm glad it's my turn."

He started to gather the dishes from the table. "Now go and get your swimming things, and be quick about it, before the Embassy ring for me again."

We walked through the streets with our arms linked, he was still nearly a head taller than me. People smiled at us and said, "Dobar dan" or "Hallo" straight away in the English – maybe they knew who we were.

It took us ages to get through the market, the sun was rising higher and people were clumping in the shade. There was a lot of shouting and laughing. The Russian ships had moved on from the harbour, and it was a beautiful day.

I had my wooden-soled sandals on, they made a wonderful noise on the cobbles. Flies wafted in the heat and fecund smells rising above the fruit and vegetables piled high on the stalls. The colours were so bright. One of the fat grannies gave me a few of her grapes.

A boy sitting cross-legged on one of the rugs he was trying to sell leapt up and grabbed my father's arm.

"Marks and Spencers?" he asked, fingering my father's silk shirt. Pale green it was, and the boy's clothes, like most peoples', were threadbare and dull. He tried to get my dad to sell him the shirt, even offered one of his rugs for it. Dad refused.

There was an ice cream stall on the edge of the beach.

"You go and find a good place," said Dad, "I'll get us ices and join you in a minute."

I'd seen his friend Ive at the stall too.

I took my sandals off and put them in the bag. My feet could feel the heat of the sun in the roughness of the rocks beneath them. I picked my way through noisy groups of Germans and Czechs, there were some Yugoslavs too. I could smell the sun-tan oil frying and the salt tang of the retreating sea. White-haloed pools lay evaporating in the deep-pitted rocks. Music was blasting in competitive stereo from various transistors dotted around the beach. 'Rube Utorake' was winning.

Our favourite place in the shadow of the rock overhang was still empty. We weren't like the tourists, wanting to get a tan to show off at home.

I laid out our towels and sat down. In the shade the sun was gentle and warm. Soaking into me. There were swifts flying curved-winged amongst the seagulls. The sea was flat and calm, you could see the pebbles, grey and rounded smooth beneath the pale green of the water. The horizon was hazy. A pale greeny blue. No clouds. It was difficult to see where the sea ended and the sky . . .

◆

"Mrs MacKinnon, Mrs MacKinnon, wake up," a voice shouted. "It's time for your medication."

Can't I even have my memories in peace?

Six

I recognised the footsteps coming ever more slowly down the corridor towards my door, and I wanted to tell him I was out. He paused outside the door and I was just beginning to allow myself to think he'd chickened out when the door slowly opened and there he was. Alasdair. He walked slowly across the corded carpet towards me, not looking at me, so I found myself looking at him more than I'd done for a long time. Difficult to believe he was only a couple of years older than me. A voice in my head, without my inviting it, told me that it was a long time since I'd looked at myself either.

His shoes were a bit grubby, his trousers a bit bagged at the knees, not much, but for him a great deal. He turned the chair slightly, so his back was more to the door, then he slumped himself into it. His balding temples were slightly shiny, and the still discernible red of the faded wisps of his curls seemed to make his face paler even than usual. There were darknesses under his eyes, and, as he glanced at me, I saw they were within them too.

I felt the great gulf between us. Between now and any time it was possible to even imagine having been close to him.

"So?" he asked.

"So-so," I replied. I turned my head to look at the trees outside the window. There was a low sinking cloud opalescent with the setting sun behind it. The naked knobbly-twigged branches were silhouetted black against it.

He was just a needy stranger I'd once known. A child with him? Unthinkable.

"Did Hartmutt not give you my message?"

"He did," I said.

"I can't remember what I said. I know I shouldn't have."

I heard him changing position in his chair, and tried to turn my head back to him. At first it wouldn't move, then it rolled back suddenly and caught us both unawares. His eyes were puffy and a little bloodshot.

He stood and re-arranged the pillows under my head so I was propped up a bit more. Touching me as if he had a right to. I didn't want him to touch me.

He sat down again. Folded his arms across his chest.

I watched the second hand on the clock on the wall over his shoulder jerking itself second by second around the yellowed face. The faint, familiar, smell of formalin came to me. Self preservation. I felt some movement in my face, a tightening, bunching up of my cheeks. I suppressed the rising giggle.

"Well," I said, "this we are good at. I haven't forgotten that at least."

He looked at me then for a moment, and there was a deepening of the dry creases at the corners of his mouth and eyes. Then he leant forward, put his hands between his knees, addressed the floor.

"Sure," he said, "things between us are terrible, even I acknowledge that now. These last weeks I've done what you've been wanting me to do, I've been forced to, to look at the way things really are. At last I agree with you."

'Not now,' I wanted to shout. 'What relevance does it have now? Everything's changed.'

He continued to gaze at the floor and all I could hear was the ticking of the clock and the fast unevenness of his breathing.

Eventually he glanced up at me, "Let's not make things worse for each other," he said, "things are bad enough. Can't we just try to sort out what's happened?"

He still doesn't believe I don't know. Didn't he ever know me at all?

"Hartmutt says she's a lovely girl," I said.

"Aye, she is."

"Then there must be something, somewhere, that's lovely in us. Or was. Mustn't there?" I immediately wished I hadn't asked.

But he didn't answer anyway.

"Alasdair," I said, "if you could just tell me what you know of what happened, perhaps we could piece it together."

"Well, I don't know," he said.

"Oh, Alasdair," I said, "never mind what they say for once. Can't we just . . .?"

But I saw that he'd moved, he was sitting straighter, looking at me.

"There was a couple," he said, "about our age. Earlier today. Their son'd come off his motor bike. Nineteen. Killed outright – the lorry driver's got a broken collar bone. They came in to identify him. His face wasn't too bad. And do you know, I found myself envying them. Isn't that terrible? And I know Sarah's not dead. I'd know if she was. But it's the not knowing. I don't know if I can stand it. You must know, you and your mother. You planned it."

"Planned it? Planned what? Planned to be like this?"

"No, of course not. That's just a reaction, and you were slightly injured, it obviously didn't go totally according to plan. But if you'd just tell me there wouldn't be any need for all this. Just tell me where she is, what she's doing. I know it's my fault too."

He looked out of the window for a moment, then back at me. "I know it's my fault," he said, and he sounded as if he really meant it.

He continued, "I shouldn't have tried to force you both to be what I wanted. Made you stay. I see that all now. And how you could feel that you had no other option. I just wanted her to have something to fall back on – be qualified for a proper job.

"You've set her up in a studio somewhere haven't you? You and your mother. With Roberto's help. He swears not, that he knows nothing about it. But he would, wouldn't he? After all it was Roberto who broke up your parents' marriage."

I wanted to protest that wasn't fair, that it was Roberto who'd helped Mum to pick up the pieces. But I took a look at the set of his face, and I didn't.

"I'm sorry," Alasdair said, "if that's what Sarah wanted to do so much I should have listened. I know things could have been so different for your mother if she'd started younger."

He blew his nose, "I'll not do anything to stop it, I'll support her. Just, for God's sake, tell me where she is, that she's all right. I won't do anything. I promise. And then you'll have no need to be like this. You or your mother."

He walked over to the window. With his back to me he said, "Am I really such a monster, that you had to resort to this? Can we be the same people we once were? I've been thinking . . . don't you remember how we once were?"

He walked back over, sat down and leaned towards me. He stroked my hand for a minute, then pulled his own back as if he'd done something he shouldn't.

He cleared his throat, but his voice was still thick. "Don't you remember how we once were?"

He turned his face away but I'd seen the glitter of the tears overspilling his eyes.

"What are you saying?" I asked, "Hartmutt's just told me I've got a daughter. And I'm trying to . . . I can't really believe that. And before I can believe that, you're telling me I haven't. That she's dead."

He leapt to his feet, "I'm telling you she's not dead," he shouted. He strode across to the window. Stood with his hands on the sill, his forehead against the glass. Rigid. His breathing, loud and uneven, filling the room.

"Horlicks, Ovaltine, or tea?"

"What?" I could feel my eyes wide glaring at the nurse.

"What would you like to drink?"

"God I don't know."

"There's no need to be like that, dear. I'll give you a cup of tea shall I?"

"Yes, thank you," I said. And I watched, without protest, as she shovelled in two heaped spoonsful of sugar. Left me my tablets in their little plastic pot.

After a couple of minutes he came back over and sat down. He saw my tablets and drink and stood again to give them to me. He wasn't concentrating, and some of the tea went down my front.

"Look," he said, when he'd sat down again, "I've been talking to Virginia. She says when people have memories that are trapped, so to speak, they can be released by using hypnosis or a truth drug," he paused. "What's the matter?"

"What's the matter?" My voice sounded sort of muffled. My teeth were clenched. "I suppose it's you asked that woman to see me, like you decided to put my mother and me in separate hospitals. What are you frightened of? That we'd make something up between us? Just what do you think we are? What do you think we've done?"

"Don't get agitated," he said, rising to his feet.

"Don't get agitated; don't get agitated?" I shouted, "who do you think you are? Arranging it all for your own benefit. I'm a person too you know. They say I'm not to be rushed. My mind'll remember when it's ready. If it's ready. Then I'll be the one who'll choose who to tell what's happened. Who do you think you are?"

I became aware of the strain in my neck and throat, could see the tea drying clinging my nightie clammily transparent to my chest, and I let my head flop back onto the pillow.

There was silence for a long time. Except for the ticking of the clock, the ragged sound of breathing, and in the distance the clattering of the drinks trolley. The television. The emptiness of professionally-cheerful voices.

He paced up and down, finally came and sat down on the side of my bed. Picked up my hand. I tried to pull it away, but I couldn't.

"Look," he said, "this is silly. I did the best I could. Who else was there?"

He went and sat down in his chair again. "You don't know what it was like. Trying to find out what'd happened. Then you turning up like that. What could I have done differently?"

"I don't know Alasdair," I said, "you don't seem to have grasped the fact that I don't know what's happened. I know less than you. I'm so sick of all these secrets, things arranged, talked about behind my back. Other people deciding what's best for me. Can't you pretend, just for a few minutes, that I'm a real person too and tell me what's happened?"

He sighed, but sat back more in the chair, seemed to be gathering his thoughts. There was some colour, now, in his cheeks.

"Well, it's really quite simple," he said. "Sarah, your mother and you set off on the 5th of December to stay with Roberto in Venice. You told us all you'd return on the 19th. I booked the tickets for you myself.

"I thought, at first, that you'd just missed the plane. Hung around the airport, tried to find out if you were booked on another flight.

39

So many people. That time of the year. Families, old friends, all around me. Loaded down with presents. Hugging and kissing each other. Laughing and talking all together. Not that it would've been like that for us anyway.

"Eventually I rang Roberto, asked whether you'd got off alright. Those terrible telephone hoods at the airport, and his thick accent. He'd been drinking. He said that you'd left on the 12th. He said that had always been the arrangement. That you would stay with him a week. He'd put you in the taxi himself.

"That's been the worst thing. The worst thing all along. This was obviously planned. You meant this to happen. Well not exactly this, obviously. But you deceived us all.

"All that time, trying to find out where you were, what had happened. You know so many people, in so many places.

"And then his phone call. That eternity later. January 15th. Roberto. I didn't think he was drunk that time. I thought he was mad. You and your mother'd turned up. No Sarah. And the way he said you were. I couldn't understand half of what he said.

"I went round to Hartmutt. That's the state I was in. Hartmutt. I knew he'd turned up for his sabbatical. Working on Hadrian's Wall – I'd have thought they'd done enough on that. He'd rung up for you just a day or two earlier, not expecting me to be there – I told him some cock and bull story.

"I rang the University. They gave me the number of his flat. He asked me round there, I couldn't have been making much sense. It's on the front, you'll like it. Overlooking the sea. He says that you're going there for Easter.

"Then he rang Roberto for me. Spoke to him in Italian. Made all the arrangements. I'd thought, in the weeks before, that I'd got to the bottom of feeling impotent. But that was it then really. In Hartmutt's flat. It wasn't him sorting it all out. It was my being grateful for it. Hartmutt. That really was the end."

He paused, remembering, smiling grimly. "And then we went together to Venice," he said, "and we brought you home.

"Those terrible stairs from Roberto's studio. I thought they'd never get your stretcher down." He wiped at his face with the back of his hand.

"We'd thought at first, that your physical injuries were worse than they've turned out to be. And your mother, they made us sedate her before they'd let us on the plane. Exhausted too, the both of you.

"That look you had in your eyes. I'd seen it before of course. Many times, can't avoid it in this sort of job. Though it's different when it's your . . . someone you . . .

"Your mother's in the right place. Don't you remember going to see her?" He looked out of the window for a moment, he was breathing hard.

"But you, they seem to think that if we can free your mind, your body will free itself too.

"You've set Sarah up in a studio somewhere, haven't you? With Roberto's help. So she can have the chance, while she's still young, the chance that your mother didn't have, to develop her painting properly.

"Roberto says she's good. I'm sorry if you felt you had to do that. She felt she had to do that."

He put his elbows on his knees, his face between his hands. He asked the floor, "Am I so unreasonable that she couldn't talk to me, if it's what she really wanted?

"Hartmutt says it's not likely that's what's happened, but I can't see what other explanation there is.

"You and Anna, you've had a road accident or something, afterwards, after you left her, and you feel guilty at deceiving me. It's alright. It's my fault too."

He straightened a little, managed to look at me. With the terrible darknesses of his eyes, looked at me.

"If you could just tell me. I could go to her. Tell her it's alright. I could help her. I'm her father.

"I love her."

Seven

I've been thinking of a time. Lying here in a great, deep, pool of calm, thinking of a time . . .

I must have been about four or five. At the school. We'd all sat cross-legged in the big ones' room – all the island children under eleven. There were nineteen of us that term because the new minister had come with his four daughters – it was more children than had gone to the school at the same time for as long as anyone could remember, and there wasn't quite enough room.

◆

The sounds of our singing were just fading from the air, and overhead we could hear again the gulls at their squawking. We could just hear the sea in its distance-subdued crashing on the shore. The wind was in the west so the lid of the stove kept lifting up and crashing back emitting great gusts of peat smoke, treacley and choking, black.

We'd all kept our coats on – just till the frost ferns and crystal patterns melted from the windows. My fingers were red and tingling, I could smell the wet wool of my gloves.

Peigi Chaimbeul tapped at her table with her ruler, but it was quite a while before Artair Mac a' Phearsain could stop coughing so we could listen to what she had to say. Iseabail Nic a' Phì had to fetch him a glass of water from the pump.

Then, sure enough, after lunch the 'Man from the Nuffield' came. He had carroty-red hair, and a beard, though his eyelashes were almost blonde. His Gàidhlig had a different sound to it, more solid round the edges somehow. Maybe he came from the North.

He came to our little ones' room.

He'd come, he said, to help us get on with our sums. Though Iseabail Nic a' Phì had always managed fine to help us by herself.

Great jigsaws he had, and lots of wooden boards. Too difficult were the jigsaws, he said, for little people such as us. They'd done a survey and the shapes and the picture you had to be older to see. But if we tried hard we could do the sums, he said – there were parts of sums on the fronts of all the pieces, and the backs of them were coloured. And if we did the sums right, put them together on a board, and, when all the pieces joined up, put a board on top, and he helped us to turn over the boards squashed together, and took off the board that had been on the bottom, but was now on the top, we'd find we'd made a beautiful picture by magic.

Me, I just made the picture – it made more sense than the sums.

He made me stand then on the table and shouted at me – in front of all the others – called me a cheat. Steaphan Sheumais pretended to drop his pencil by me so he could crawl on the floor and look up my skirt. I was wearing my green gym knickers.

✦

On my way home, I remember, I'd sat, for a while, huddled in my little hollow amongst the pink-tipped buds of the dog-roses. I couldn't understand what wrong it was I had done.

The picture I'd made then had been beautiful.

I found my eyes going again to the window. But there was still just the knobbly black twigs – and the sky.

I remember, when I'd finally arrived home my mother'd been painting, and I'd got into trouble again getting the paint on my fingers, smudging her sky, as I'd tried to ease the canvas forward to see if she had sums on the back of it.

I'd become even more confused trying to explain it to her. We'd sat on the floor before the fire, and she'd read me a story from the myths and legends book – shape-changers and the salmon of knowledge – then she'd let me watch as, back at her easel, she turned my soily smudge into a seagull high soaring in flight.

Such a long time it was before I'd understood that what the stupid man should have told me was how good I was with the shapes and with the picture.

43

Though it was the pictures that words made in my head which interested me in the end. And the pictures in other people's heads, which never seemed to be just the same.

Virginia. Can you imagine a mother looking at a red, wrinkled, bawling scrap of a thing and deciding to call it Virginia? Though she's got it right fair enough. Sure, it's herself that's repressed. She's just projecting it onto me.

I'm so tired, so tired. No visitors, they said, for forty eight hours. As if they imagine looking at black, knobbly twigs and the grey of the sky was good for me. I closed my eyes, and I must have slept, for I dreamt. Of Virginia. Though is it a dream when recent events just replay themselves in your head? I don't know. Anyway, that's what happened. Again and again as if it were on a loop.

✦

"My dear woman this sort of thing is hardly without precedent, you know. A woman of your age, with the type of restrictive, not to say repressive, upbringing you had. It will out. The religious aspect too – that part of Scotland, might as well be Ireland, might it not?

"And your only child about to fly the nest. I hesitate to call it classic, but – my dear . . .

"And, then, there's the death of your father in Zagreb, two years ago now, is it? And your guilt that you haven't, because of the political situation there, been to sort out his affairs which he'd entrusted to you. He was obviously an important factor in your life, perhaps too much so. One of your preoccupations with memories of Yugoslavia obviously stems from that. That and, as I've already mentioned, the metaphor for breakdown. The mind does tend thus to be economical, especially when it is, if I may say so, somewhat limited in what it has available to it with which to work.

"And there's your still problematical relationship with Dr MacKinnon. The seeming inability you share to let go of something you both see as long dead. Interesting, in that respect, his choice of career as a pathologist."

✦

I turned to the window again, sighing. Lights were coming on in the far distance, so it must be the gray of the gloaming now, not the gray that's been with us for most of the day.

She doesn't understand the first thing about my life.

Maybe she does.

Perhaps I've done something terrible and she knows. Why else would she be like that?

I could see the dampness hanging in the air, swirling a little – there must be a breeze.

What have I done?

Haloes of light grew and brightened around the street lights and the damp drifted into them seeping them with rainbow hues.

Alasdair, I learnt with you what love could be. Perhaps we should have known that such intensity could only be fleeting.

Yes, Alasdair, I remember how we once were. And isn't it just that remembering that's kept us clinging together long past the time we should have moved on? Before the present began to poison the past, the future.

Eight

Ripples, ripples reaching me in the deep place where I was. I felt myself floating upwards, saw a familiar shape standing by me.

Hartmutt, gradually coming into focus.

He looked so solid and real, then as he bent towards my face and I heard him kiss me, but felt only the vague light warmth of him, I realised he wasn't. Or I wasn't, one of the two.

He sat in his chair and I watched him pick up my hand. He raised that to his lips too, but that I couldn't feel at all.

He straightened his legs and sat back in the chair. He looked relaxed. The break from visiting had done him good anyway.

"Hartmutt, do you remember the words of 'Ruby Tuesday'?"

"'Ruby Tuesday'?"

"Yes, you know, 'Rube Utorake', they were playing it all the time the summer we met."

"Oh, yes, the Rolling Stones wasn't it? I was more of a Beatles man myself," he said. "Have you been thinking of then again? I've got some very fond memories of that time too."

He hummed hesitantly to himself for a minute or two, then sang quietly, "Goodbye, Rube Utorake". He repeated the phrase, then stopped again frowning. "However did it go?" he asked.

He tried again, "Hallo, Ruby Tuesday" he sang. Then he laughed, shaking his head, "I don't know, love, sorry."

"It doesn't matter," I said.

He looked at me as if measuring me up. "Why do you think it is," he asked, "that your thoughts seem to keep returning to so far back?"

"Virginia says Yugoslavia is my metaphor for breakdown," I told him.

He sat up a little straighter. "You think she's wrong?"

"Well," I said, "you all seem to think that I think that on principle."

He smiled, but didn't deny it.

"Yes," I said, "I think she's wrong. It's just safe, isn't it? The past. I survived that. She's determined to make something out of nothing. Though to be fair, I do know I'm not giving her a lot to go on. I don't have a lot to go on."

I looked at him, "It's just a place, a time, of happy memories."

"But, my dear, it's twenty-nine, thirty, years ago," he smiled wryly, "don't you have any more recent memories that are happy?"

"Yes, you know I have. Some wonderful memories, some of them you share."

"You'll survive this too, love, just you wait and see."

"How can you say that," I asked him, "when you don't know what's happened?"

"I know you."

"Hartmutt," I said, "I'm scared." I saw him pick up my hand again, hold it between both of his own. "I didn't realise it till just now. I'm frightened to remember."

"I don't blame you."

"Aren't you supposed to tell me that there's nothing to be frightened of?"

"I might have done, all those years ago. You were frightened of the submarines in the bay, I remember that."

He was quiet for a moment, as if he was wondering whether he should tell me something. Eventually he said, "my own earliest memories are of fear."

I saw his eyes go distant with remembering.

He cleared his throat. "I was five or so at the end of the Second World War," he said. "All my earliest memories are of under a table, the bombs falling, my mother whimpering. Time and again throughout my life people have tried to make me feel guilty for being a German, as if the War were my fault.

"My contribution to the War was to cower under a table, clinging to my mother, wetting myself."

We were both silent for a while, he wasn't seeing me. I'd never met his mother, never heard him speak of her before.

He moved in his seat and took a deep breath in. He looked at me. "I don't know why you didn't tell the truth about how long you were going to stay with Roberto," he said. "I don't know what you intended to do in that week you planned to be missing. But I know you. Clearly it hasn't gone as it was supposed to. But I simply cannot believe you planned anything that you need be frightened of knowing. Of remembering."

He looked at me, his eyes dark. "But there's Sarah, love."

"Sarah?" I asked.

"Yes, I can't help thinking she's somewhere alone, waiting for us to contact her."

"Oh, God, I never thought of that. How awful. I still somehow don't think of her as real."

We were both silent for a while.

"But, Hartmutt, why hasn't she contacted us?"

"We're none of us where she'd expect us to be," he said. "I stayed with Alasdair for a couple of nights in your house in case she rang, but neither of us could stand it. We have left the answering machine on, but it's occurred to me that she'd not leave a message on it if she were avoiding Alasdair, if she wanted to speak only to you."

"Where's he staying now then?"

"In the doctors' residence at the Infirmary."

"This keeps getting worse."

"No, love, it doesn't. This is the way it's been for some time. And we're getting closer to being able to do something about it. Of course you're scared. But you'll not let that stop you doing something about it. I know that. It's just a question of time now."

"Are you working up to asking me for a reference as cheerleader?"

"What, with my legs?"

And I looked at them, not at their best, spread on the chair straining the seams of his cords.

But after he'd gone my mind blanked again, and I just lay for a while till I drifted off to sleep.

✦

Jane was leaning over me shouting something. I struggled to open my eyes. She looked flushed and self-important.

"Hallo, sleeping beauty," she said, "Today is your lucky day."

I looked at the nurse standing beside her. She looked even younger than Jane, and very thin.

"This is Ellen," said Jane, "We're going to give you a bath in the Parker. I'm going to show Ellen how it's done."

"Oh, good," I said.

She pushed a wheelchair round to the side of the bed, and put its brakes on.

"What's the Parker?" I asked.

"It's a bath sort of like a seat, and we can tip it back once you're in," said Jane. "Shows how pleased with you they are that they're letting you get up to have a bath."

"The side comes down like a guillotine," said Ellen helpfully.

"Yes," said Jane, "it lifts up so that it's easier to get you in, then we have to close it properly, or all the water comes out when we tip you back."

"Sounds like fun," I said.

"You'll be alright," said Jane, "we do know what we're doing, you know."

"I'm sure you do, Jane," I said.

But it seemed that, having to concentrate to explain to someone else, she did. They humoured me whilst I made a joke about a tumbril as they, skilfully enough, except in hiding the effort, manoeuvred me into the wheelchair. They even seemed to listen whilst I explained what a tumbril was, and, during the ride to the bathroom, gave a short talk on the French Revolution.

And, sure enough, they managed fine. And so did I. Lying in my bed I hadn't known the extent of the helplessness of my body. The muscles were already flabby and wasted looking.

Trying to help them I learnt how weak I was, how easily exhausted, and out of breath.

Aye, we managed fine, but it wasn't a body I recognised as mine. It wasn't a body whose present state I was prepared to go on accepting as mine.

Nine

And I'm remembering now another bath.

Green marble it was. I'd never been in a bathroom like it. The bath was a mottle of green, and the taps gold. I'd lain and moved my hand slowly, infinitesimally, up and down so the water shivered and the light on it shimmered as if the marble had liquefied silky warm around me. Plants in primitive pots trailed and climbed and sprawled, multiply reflected in the mirrored walls, so it seemed like a vast garden. I even looked, once or twice, for the gardener.

Water embryo warm, moist smells of soil and skin. Reflections of reflections. Ferns, fronds, uncurling.

And in the bedroom beyond Hartmutt singing. Off-key, unsure of the words, with great gusto.

✦

We'd left at 4am that morning so we'd arrive, he'd said, before the heat of the day grew too intense. Sure, we might have done too, if we hadn't dawdled so much on the way. It was barely light and we ate the last of the blackberries from the bushes on the climb up the track to the road. Some of the gaunt white cows staggered to their feet, bells hollowly clanking, as we disturbed them from their dreams.

We drove down into Assisi, and on, peering at the landscape insubstantial and surreal through the haze of the dawning and the dust cloud churned up by our wheels. In time we were joined on the road by other cars, but they were in their clouds too, and the feeling of being alone in a world that wasn't quite material didn't pass.

We didn't speak. Hartmutt just drove and drove. Mid-morning

we began to look for somewhere to stop. The fields of sunflowers were just beginning to turn to seed. So, feeling like Gulliver, we stopped in their shade for lunch. Hartmutt picked some figs from the roadside bushes, and we ate them as they were, fat and stickily dusty, with our ciabiatta and black olives and cheese.

He lay on his back then, with his hat over his face, and noisily slept. I lay and watched the heat-bleached blue of the sky through the long swaying golden petals of the mammoth-headed flowers. The edges of some of them were just beginning to dry and curl.

When we awoke we resumed our journey, but great crowds had found Capo de Monte before us, and our progress was slowed to a crawl. We managed to battle our way through the narrow streets and on to the lake-side and eventually we even found somewhere to park.

At the jetty was the speedboat Domenico had sent for us – it was manned by the Ancient Mariner himself. The engine of the speedboat had been hyped up and it seemed to stand in the water, bouncing from wave to wave. Not that they could really be called waves, except those we left in our wake.

The Mariner said, with great pride, that he'd worked on the engine himself. A teenager still, in the leathery, creased body of an old man.

However, we broke up the water's reflection of the sun, and made a fine breeze. It was almost cool. We couldn't talk above the motor-bike roar of the engine, and the thud of our contact with the waves. We clung to the bow rail. The metal of it was surprisingly cold. Some of the time I felt as if I were flying, my face uplifted to the blue of the sky, my hair streaming out behind me. Some of the time I was scared we were going to flip over. The spray of our passing kaleidoscoped rainbows.

Hartmutt had to give me his hand to help me land, my legs were shaky. Domenico came down to meet us. To meet Hartmutt. He gave us a drink, showed us quickly around then they went off so he could show Hartmutt what he'd uncovered in his monastery. Ask his opinion.

I'd decided to have a bath and then, maybe, to wander around for a while on my own before joining them for dinner under the trees as we'd agreed.

✦

I could hear Hartmutt singing. He wasn't sure of the words.

I lay, listening, still half-asleep, in the soft warmth of the water. There were moist smells of soil and skin. Plants and their reflections were echoed again and again in the mirrors of the walls. Difficult to be sure which were real. I wasn't sure where I was.

The water shivered and the light on it shimmered as if the marble had liquefied silky warm around me. I floated my arm to the surface of the water. My arm wouldn't break through. The marble was solidifying, I wouldn't be able to move.

I must have cried out for Hartmutt came running. He helped me out and hugged me to him as I was, warm and dripping and confused. At first I couldn't clear the feeling from my mind, a deja vu sort of feeling, that I didn't quite understand.

He left me in bed to have a bath himself. I must have drifted off back into a dreamless sleep, for there he was again, in his disreputable old towelling dressing gown, sitting on the side of the bed. He was warm and pink and smelled of sandalwood. He had something concealed in one of his hands.

"I have something for you," he said.

I half-propped myself up on my elbow and tried to see what he had in his hand. Whatever it was it was small and wrapped in white tissue paper.

"What is it?" I asked.

"Oh, you have to guess," he said.

I unwrapped it as it lay in his hand, and I was glad he'd be thinking I was trying to guess, for it didn't seem to be much of a present to be giving at all and I didn't know just what to say.

There were five pieces in all, two small grey mottled pebbles shaped like pear-drops, another, of similar shape, of a grey sandy concrete stuff, two others of the same material, slightly bigger, flatter shards, uneven. One side of one of the bigger pieces was covered in black pigment, the other had one side half black, half red, with the grey showing through in the centre. Bright colours. Like pieces of a jigsaw. They looked cheap and flimsy. He knew I wasn't an archaeologist. How could he expect me to know what they were?

"I don't know, Hartmutt. Definitely not a Grecian Urn."

I looked to him, but he was clearly determined not to give me a clue. Maybe it's something Domenico's just given him, though it doesn't look as if it's come from a Franciscan monastery either. Most of the colours I'd seen as he showed us round had been the usual lambent blues and greys.

"Have you got it just now?"

"No," he said, "it seems a long time ago already, though its only about nine months isn't it? A new year, a new decade. I thought of you then. And of Marie, of course. You were such a good friend to me then – during her illness, her death. Its aftermath.

"You always have been. A good friend, I mean. But I'd always felt so much older than you, as if I had to look out for you. But during that time it changed, or I realised it had, anyway.

"Life goes on, they say. Not true. But for some it starts again. Eventually.

"The third anniversary of her death. Time to begin anew. And I thought of you."

He turned the coloured pieces over in his hands. "Of course, they're all over the place now, being sold even, cheapened somehow. But these pieces are real."

"They're part of the Berlin Wall aren't they?" I asked.

"Yes," he said, "from the part just to the right of the Brandenberg gate. Enough pieces being sold now for the whole of Germany to have been walled – rooved – over."

We both smiled.

"But these pieces are real," he said again.

I took them from him, turned them over in my hands, so light they were. I wasn't sure what it was he was trying to say.

"All of Europe was there," he said. "New year 1990. I'd spent the last two alone. From one extreme to the other."

He pulled the duvet over his legs, and I moved over so he could get in beside me.

"All the West was singing and they were passing round seemingly endless bottles of champagne. Shaking the bottles so it spurted all over – you know. Most had clearly had a lot to drink already. I didn't feel quite a part of it. So perhaps I was one of the few to notice that the East was strangely silent. They were not facing the West. They were facing the Brandenberg gate. There were people on top of the Wall. Westerners. Jumping. At midnight the West put down the flag and put up the European flag. The Westerners were cheering, hugging, shouting. But the Easterners, they booed.

"It was as if they didn't want the tide of history to wash them away. They just wanted to be themselves. Well, that's how it seemed to me." He put his arm around my shoulder, and I snuggled down into him.

"Marie came from Berlin, you know," he said, "her family were split by it. Even when it became clear that her cancer was terminal many of them were unable to visit her."

He was silent for a while.

"We talked such a lot in those last months," he said. "It was horrific at times, watching her die like that – so little that I could do – but somehow, it was then we were closest." He cleared his throat.

"Then, that night at the Wall, I mean, the East Berliners aren't Europeans, but they were helpless in the tide of History. I wish I could explain it better, the different feelings that were there then.

"The coming down of the Wall has come to be a symbol of freedom for others," he said, "but for them it was the loss of the freedom to be themselves. Politicians, people, they're not the same."

He paused again. "Then, somehow, that was forgotten, and they all swarmed over, and everyone was hugging and kissing, laughing. Breaking it down. I was swept up in it too, for a while. I wish I could tell you what it really felt like – the energy, the joy, of it. I really felt I was part of something. For a while. Then I went home.

"People need to feel part of something. I suppose that's why we're so easy to manipulate. One of the reasons anyway."

He took the pieces from me again, wrapped them up and put them on the bedside table.

"Have you decided," he asked, "what you're going to do?"

"But Sarah's only eleven," I said, "that's the age I was when I left the island. When we ceased to be a family. She's a different person to me, the circumstances are different. But I know what that has meant to me."

"So?" he asked quietly.

"No," I said, "I haven't made up my mind."

We dressed and walked down to the shore. The fierce heat of the day was subsiding and the birds were singing again. We walked slowly down the winding slope of the crazy paving path through the burgeoning of the garden. Palm trees, and mimosa, flowers of every hue and size, few I could name. And the low, sandstone walls whose purpose had probably been to keep them in. We passed the segmented wheel of the herb garden, down the carved stone steps and through the long grass following our ears to the sounds of the lapping of the lake.

Trees overhanging the water were drooping Narcissus-like. We sat on the bank under them with our feet on the rocks. We sat and watched as the sun set into the lake flaring the sky and water orange, and the gently lacing hem of the water lapped slowly over our toes, gradually upwards, to our ankles. We waited till the sun had sunk quite into the water, beyond the water, then he took my hand and we walked back to Domenico and the trestle table set under the trees by the side of the monastery.

We had pasta and salad and courgette flowers coated in batter and deep fried. And red wine.

Then Domenico took us into the underground passages beneath the monastery he was restoring. He'd hidden there, he said, with his mother during the Second World War. He'd have said more if Hartmutt hadn't been there. Or if I hadn't. But I saw the narrow worn steps, and the damp dark widenings of the underground passage, the calender marked off on the wall. And perhaps there wasn't an awful lot to be said.

That night our need for each other, to each other, was so great that I was afraid, once or twice, in fleeting moments of outer awareness, that Domenico would hear us.

Eventually Hartmutt went for orange juice. It felt very cold and sharp in my throat. The stars were already fading though the lightening of the sky was as yet imperceptible. He got back into bed beside me.

"So," he said, "you've decided."

I even smiled, feeling the long explanations I'd agonised over drifting away, unuttered.

"Yes," I said, "I've decided.

I turned my head into his chest so I couldn't see him, but I could still hear the raggedness of his breathing. Feel it.

"She'd think it was her fault," I said.

He didn't say anything.

"Just till she's a bit older, more secure in herself . . ." I cleared my throat. "Foundations can't be added after . . .

"So long to get over – if ever, completely . . . make it so difficult for her to do better."

We lay in silence and stroked one another. With gentleness now. As the sun rose inexorably.

"I can't ask . . ." I said.

"I can't promise . . ." he said.

After breakfast Domenico took us on a final tour to admire his restoration of the monastery, then took us back to the speedboat. Hartmutt had already seen the best bits, and it was difficult to think of anything sufficiently encouraging to say. Though the frescos were beautiful, the colours being brought back to life. But I was aware, mostly, of the walls that were being rebuilt.

Ten

Italy 1990. How long ago that seems. But he was right, Hartmutt, wasn't he? A forced marriage that hasn't worked. Of the East and the West at Berlin. At least that's how it seems. How it's reported.

Our marriage certainly wasn't forced. Mine and Alasdair's. It had been so wonderful to find him. Someone who understood where I was coming from. Who was ahead of me in where we thought we were going.

And so much in love. Then.

Sure, if things'd been different, things would have been different. And for Hartmutt and me too. Can we ever, with certainty, say more than that?

I'm just thinking words. It doesn't solve anything.

That last evening with Hartmutt, we'd gone to the piazza in Assisi. Still warm it was and we'd had wine at a table that'd still had it's umbrella on. There'd been a crescent moon, and a choir was standing on the steps, singing. There were more people out, sitting, strolling, than there ever were in the heat of day. There's maybe something about living in countries such as that – the sun unfolds a different part of the nature of people than the cold and the wind augments in the Scots. Though we endure.

Is that always a good thing?

I tried again to think of her, imagine her – this daughter of mine that I still couldn't drag up from the frozen depths of my memory. But something had changed – I knew, now, that she was in there – somewhere.

But whenever I tried to make an image of her, or think of how she might be feeling, my mind seemed to bounce off. I activated not memory, but great rising swirls of anxiety. Fear.

I managed to wriggle my bell push out from under the pillow and got my thumb to it.

"Well, hallo," said Jane as she appeared, slightly out of breath, by my side, "I didn't know you could press that."

"There wouldn't seem to be much point, then, in giving it to me."

She stepped back slightly, I'd spoken much too sharply.

"Well," she said, "it makes people feel better, doesn't it? And we do check on you all the time." She looked at her watch, "Anyway, what can I do for you?"

"I'm sorry for snapping," I tried to speak slowly, not to sound impatient. "Would you open the window for me please?"

"The window? But you'll freeze to death, you're still not well, can't you see the snow?"

"But, Jane, the air in here, it's so hot, recycled so many times, all the life breathed out of it. How can I get better if I can't breathe in the fresh air?"

"Well, alright," she said, "maybe if I did it just on the first hole."

After she'd gone I lay, trying to feel, imagine I felt, a breeze on my face, a freshening of the air. Eventually I succeeded, though whether it was a success of feeling or imagination I didn't just know.

✦

"Now, Mrs MacKinnon, I think today must be the day we say 'enough'."

Back in my bed I listened to the recorded low-lights of my bout with Virginia replay themselves in my head.

"It's not beyond comprehension that you should feel some resentment for the way your life has become, though I feel I really must point out your own complicity in this. But to continue to project the blame for it onto Dr MacKinnon, to punish him for it by with-holding information about his daughter, though, again, understandable, has really got beyond what we can continue to permit.

"Though I've made different choices in my own life, not without certain sacrifices, don't imagine that I don't understand the positions of women like your mother and yourself.

"Let's just sum up the situation.

"Your mother sacrificed the full flowering of her artistic abilities, to be with the man she loved as he recovered, back in the island retreat of his forefathers, from the trauma of his brush with reality during the end of the Second World War. I can appreciate the charm of that. And her rage when he recovered.

"We all role-play to a certain extent, are understandably put out when someone else changes that we assumed a life-long script.

"Your own rage is all-too evident. Though that too is understandable. You obviously stayed in a defunct marriage because you knew only too well the effect of a split on a lone child. Maybe you feel that your husband, with mixed motives, emotionally blackmailed you into making that choice. And, in truth, that may be so. But what is clear is that you feel that you have been sacrificed both to your parents and to your own child.

"And there's the death of your father, clearly not an entirely healthy relationship, more unfinished business, which, whether you've been aware of it or not, will have taken its toll.

"We cannot change the past. Only learn from it.

"And at some level you know that to blame and punish your husband, as scapegoat, for all this is simply not on. And your mother knows that too. And with the enclosed, religious milieu of your upbringing, you'll both have majored in guilt, as it were.

"So, you've inflicted a little, minor injury on yourself, and an hysterical mental condition, with considerable somatic overlay, as a form of punishment. You may, even, have engineered a minor accident to, seemingly, validate this self-inflicted punishment.

"All this is self-evident.

"But the time has come, my dear lady, to put this all behind us. To face up to the reality of the situation, and move on from it.

"And, if I may presume to mention, to think of the effect all this is having on your daughter.

"You must beware of projecting these things onto your daughter, and of using her as a pawn in your still problematical relationship with her father. Interesting, in that respect, his choice of career as a pathologist.

"You must beware, your mother and yourself, of projecting onto Sarah your own disappointments and inadequacies. You must allow her to make her own life choices, even if you so strongly feel, as you both obviously do, that you have yourselves been denied this basic human right. Beware, these things do tend to be inherited, generation after generation, together with the colour of the eyes, and the imperviousness to good advice.

"The poor girl, no wonder she hasn't made contact since Venice. If she's any sense she'll stay holed up until she's come to her own arrangements.

"A fascinating machine – the mind. Its ability to somatically reflect its own condition is without parallel. If we could just get your mind to acknowledge and move on, then your body could follow suit."

✦

Then I remembered my fellow patient, awaiting his turn in the waiting room whilst she confided my finer points to her tape-recorder, and I sat ready for a porter to return me to my bed. I suppose he'd seen, and recognised, identified with, something in the expression of my face.

"Oh her," he'd said, "what she needs is a good fuck."

✦

I was so engrossed in my self-inflicted exercises that I heard the banging shut of the window before I realised Alasdair was in the room. I flopped my head back the good centimetre or so I'd managed to lift it off the bed – insufficient still to see if I was actually moving my toes or not, but there was definitely an ache – some sort of sensation – in the back of my calves. And in my neck.

"How was Virginia?" Alasdair asked, walking back across the room towards me.

"Herself," I said.

He gave a tut of irritation, "Has it not occurred to you," he asked, "that she's maybe trying to provoke you into some sort of action, reaction, some signs of life?"

"Then she's as little understanding of my situation as yourself."

He sighed, "I'm sorry."

He wasn't, but I didn't think it was worth the hassle either.

"Alasdair," I said, "I've been thinking."

He laughed, albeit a little hollowly, "Well, that makes a change," he said, and sat down in his chair, leaning forward, "Stuck here in that bed you've been doing far too much of it, if you ask me. I suppose, to be fair, it is difficult for you to keep things in proportion. God knows it's difficult enough for me, and I've got far too much else to occupy my mind just now."

"You seem better for it."

"Yes, things do seem a bit clearer today."

"Alasdair, do you think they'd let me go and see my mother?"

"What now?"

"Yes, now. As you say I could do with a change, maybe a different perspective on things."

He leapt up, "I'll go and see what I can arrange."

He paused in the doorway, turned and smiled. "It's such a relief to see you wanting to do something, I can't tell you."

Did she really say all that? Virginia.

He returned with a rug. "All arranged," he said, "some nurses will be here directly with a wheelchair."

"That was quick," I said, "I wouldn't have thought they'd think me safe to let loose."

"Not all the strings I pull are of elastic," he said.

But the arrival of Jane and Ellen with the wheelchair cut short my retort.

✦

"Alasdair, do you remember the words of 'Ruby Tuesday'?" I asked.

He frowned out through the windscreen for a while, then said, "Something about, 'Goodbye,' and hanging names on people. Then, later, . . . still they're going to get you. I don't know, I can't think of any more. What do you want to know for anyway?"

"It's just a song," I said, "It keeps going round in my head, you know how it is."

The traffic was quite heavy, and I was pleased enough just to watch the world go by, let him concentrate on his driving. I felt quite comfortable, glad to be out, though strange enough it was too be sure. Even cocooned in the car it seemed a different, brighter, but strangely alien world.

I can't have been in a car crash, can I? or I wouldn't feel safe riding in a car now.

The roads were clear, though there were still some sludges of snow on the verges. So much sky, and in places you could imagine blue in the grey of it. It could almost give you agoraphobia, if you weren't so amazingly well-adjusted.

"Alasdair," I asked, "How long have you known Virginia?"

"Oh, I don't know," he said. "Are you warm enough?"

Then we were pulling up at the red-brick building. Victorian, by the look of it, like the hospital we'd just left. Though I must say I prefer them to the modern type, so cluttered and public and inhuman somehow. He got me into my wheelchair and soon we were in a long, low corridor. There seemed to be something familiar about it. They said they'd brought me here to see her once before though I'd no recollection of it. Maybe the familiarity was just of the sameness of the many hospitals Alasdair'd worked in, rather than this once itself. I didn't like the idea I'd been somewhere and didn't know anything about it. I was nervous about how my mother would be. Though they'd told me what to expect.

Then he wheeled me into a sort of day room. There were chairs around the four walls of it, and people sitting in most of them. Some talking to themselves, one man muttering angrily, thumping the arm of his chair. You could see his urine-bag bulging out of the top of his sock. Most of them were just sitting, immobile, staring into space. Or at something they'd rather not see.

Then Mum wandered in. She didn't see us at first. She was looking at the floor and muttering, twisting the hem of her skirt in her hands. Her legs were bare. I remembered I had seen her like this before. Alasdair and I'd quarrelled, she'd been singing. She looked up and noticed us, took a step back, her hand going to her mouth. Then she looked again, and I saw some sort of recognition in her eyes.

"Hallo, Mum," I said.

She took another step further from us.

Alasdair took a step forward, held out his hand.

She put her hands in her pockets, looked at the floor, but "Hallo, Alasdair," she said.

He took us to a conservatory where it was quieter, just people coming for a wander now and again. There was one old man who kept coming just for a couple of puffs of a cigarette. He struck his match cupped in his hands, and smoked the same way, looking around him. The smell hung in the air, acrid and choking. Doesn't he know how dangerous it is?

Mum wouldn't stay still for long, though Alasdair managed to get her to stop every now and again, to speak directly to him – though not always saying anything that made sense. I found myself struggling to make sense of the words. Gàidhlig was my first language, had been my first language, and I found myself struggling now to make sense of what she was saying. Though to be sure it didn't have much sense to it. But I concentrated only on her words.

To myself she spoke not at all. She barely looked at me. She didn't want to look at me.

In the car on the way back I decided to brush up on my Gàidhlig, it seemed like a part of me that somehow I'd lost. I told him that, so we stopped at our house and he went in to get some books for me. He was pleased, almost enthusiastic, he said it would give me something more constructive to do, take my mind off myself, so the visit had done some good, at least for him.

As I waited for him I found myself reciting the multiplication tables. Anything to stop myself thinking of my mother. To still the waves of panic which seemed just under the surface of my mind. I was saying them in the English, though I never had at school.

He got back in, dumped my post on my lap, some books on the back seat, and drove off with hardly a glance at me.

"We're invited to supper with Hartmutt before I take you back, if you feel up to it. So much excitement in one day," Alasdair said when I noticed we'd taken the coast road and not that towards the safety of my bed. "It'll give you a chance to see where you're going at Easter. That's not so far off now."

"Did you arrange that just today?" I asked.

"Yes," he said, putting his foot down on the gas, "I thought we might as well since we were out. Should I have mentioned it earlier?" He overtook, making the oncoming driver slow down, "I phoned from the hospital while you were with your mum. Not much notice for him, it'll probably be sauerkraut sandwiches."

"He's a far better cook than you'll ever be."

"I've not needed to be until recently," he said.

We were just a few minutes away from Hartmutt's flat before he asked me if I wanted to go.

Hartmutt seemed a little anxious too when he came out to the car to meet us. He must have been watching out for us. The flat was on the top floor, of course, of a lovely sandstone Victorian crescent. But there was a lift, and I supposed they could get me downstairs between them in the event of fire.

It was a flat like any temporary university flat anywhere. A bit institutional, impersonal. Just Hartmutt's mud – or Hadrian's was it? – on the floor to give it any sense of home.

The floor boards in the centre of the room were decayed and springy, you could see the movement when Hartmutt or Alasdair walked over them, smell the smell of decay. I could hear the men talking, but I spent most of the time looking out of the window. At the sea. It seemed so long since I'd seen the sea.

If I listened hard I could just hear the sounds of the sea, of the wind. Or was it imagination just? I felt heavy and hollow with the tiredness of me. Unreal.

Eleven

I wasn't aware of leaving the flat. Just of the two men helping the nurses get me back into bed. Of Alasdair apologising. Jane's indignant voice, later, as she took my temperature and pulse.

"Poor woman," she said, "look at the state of her – I thought he was supposed to be a doctor."

It felt good to be in bed. Looked after.

Long time since I'd felt like that. When?

✦

I was in bed, safe and warm. The tented covers blanketed my world. The torch light flickered, illuminating a disc of the words in the book propped against my pillow. The book they'd given me for my eleventh birthday. It was the fattest one I'd ever had, I'd still not finished it. My breath reflected back at me warm from the pages. The music, with its background of static, was – from long practice – just quieter than my mother's approaching footsteps.

I quickly turned the radio off, and the torch, shoved them and the book under the pillow, managed to be lying flat just as she opened the door. She came in and rearranged the covers carefully – so as not to wake me – she kissed my forehead. Then she went out.

After a while I made my cocoon again to deaden the noise. In the black, damp-wool darkness I listened to the radio, but I didn't try to read again. Joan Baez, the Beatles with 'She loves you', and 'I want to hold your hand'.

I was just beginning to drift off when I was suddenly awake, there was a silence, eerie and loud. Then in hushed tones they made an announcement. President Kennedy had been shot. They talked confusedly for a while, then said they were going off the air. So I switched the radio off. It seemed so immensely shocking that such a thing should have been able to reach me, touch me, in the safety of my bed, in my parents' house, on our island.

Suddenly, for the first time, the world seemed too close, uncontrollable. And the blankets seemed no longer to be a cocoon but a barrier, letting the world into me but preventing me being part of it. The beyond was heard, but not seen. Untouchable.

And there was a terrible noise, snake hissing, maybe it was from just outside the blankets, I lay all night too frightened to move. Under the blankets I found it hard to breathe, but I couldn't move.

In the morning, of course, I found that the hissing had been static just. I'd not turned the radio off, just moved the waveband off the station.

✦

I opened my eyes to the soiled pink of my hospital room, but I was smiling. That had happened, all those years ago, of course. But all that fear for nothing.

And I wonder how much of the memory of that night is still with me for itself and how much because of the events around that time which I later came to associate with it. Because it had been only a few weeks after that night that my life changed from what it had always been to the first of the succession of things it was to become.

There'd been the bewildering noise and the crowds of school, the strange accents. My parents were abroad, so I couldn't go home at the weekends. I'd thought they'd always be there for me. My place in the way of things there for me. And, suddenly, that wasn't so.

There were all the hard paved streets, and the traffic. And at night there were lights in the houses and the streets, so I couldn't see the stars. I had to wear shoes all the time. And there was an over-whelming mixture of smells and the noise. It was too far from the sea.

And Dad, finally recovered from his shell-shock, they said, went back to his studies. Then to his succession of Embassies, being taken over by the talking, soothing, smoothing. No longer quite the man I knew. Later I came to see it as the positive side of the illness caused by his experiences of war. But not then.

How could I?

And there was Mum, a little lost, trailing round after him at first. Then beginning to do something about her painting. Exhibiting. Meeting Roberto.

But I survived.

I did more than survive. I made the life I wanted. The life I used to want.

But all that fear, for nothing. And I'm wondering, just, if it's the same thing that I'm doing now.

And I slept. I slept a lot after that. And some of the time I didn't dream at all.

Twelve

And Easter already and I'm in Hartmutt's flat again.

He came from the bedroom knotting his tie just as the record on his pre-historic player came mercifully to a close. I don't know why even he thinks now that I should be bombarded with noise. 'Stimulated.' It turns me right off.

He looked a little unfamiliar – there are so few times I've seen him wearing a suit. His wedding, Marie's funeral. I prefer him in his cords and jumpers – and the boots that've trampled archaeologically significant mud into so many of my carpets in so many different parts of the world.

He glanced at me on his way over to the mirror.

"You're thinking you wish you were coming? There's still time – I can help you." He pulled his tie undone. "I can stay."

"No, Hartmutt, really," I told his back as he pulled his tie further round his neck so the knot would be fatter and began to tie it again. Its sludgy green matched his suit – Marie must have bought it for him.

"Always, since I came back, there've been people with me, or likely to be with me any minute. Questions, tests, never leaving me alone. I've been so looking forward to these couple of hours."

He came over and kissed me on the forehead before disappearing into the kitchen. He forgot to avoid the floorboards in the centre of the room and they creaked alarmingly as they recovered from his passing.

I turned slightly in the chair to look through the window at the sea. There was a cold greyness to it. The wind was getting up.

He came back carrying a red vacuum flask and a mug and put them on the little table beside me. He moved the phone a little closer. He put the remote control on top of my book. He straightened my rug and tucked it in.

"Hartmutt, will you not just go?"

He looked at me still uncertain. I moved my hand to touch his sleeve, I couldn't reach his hand. He straightened.

"I won't be late. Ten thirty – eleven o'clock maybe."

"Don't get too drunk, I'll not be able to carry you to bed."

But when the door closed behind him it seemed strange to be alone. Strangely silent. Then the creaks and settlings of the house became over-loud. I clicked the TV on and flicked from channel to channel. They were all showing frenetic quiz shows and soaps that seemed to be from another planet. Though I knew it was myself that was the alien. I turned them all off.

I moved again in my chair so I could watch the sea. There was much white now as the waves curled and broke foaming. The moon was close to full, and the sky already darkening enough so the stars showed. A fishing boat, shaped like a moccasin, bravely – or foolishly – moved slowly northwards, the canvas of its awning rhythmically illuminated red, then faded to a darker shade of grey in a grey world as the beam from the lighthouse rotated.

And suddenly, in my mind, I'm home.

✦

And the sun is warm to the top of my head. The sea is cold to my feet, surging up to my knees. Foaming. The sand, as I step, grittily squidges up between my toes, round the edges of my feet, sinking me into it. The sea gulls call, and the wind soughs in the sea-ward slant of the blossom-laden trees and petals scatter with their fragrance on the air, float on the salt tang of the waves. Pink. By the seaweed-greened rocks the grey heads of the seals bob dark-eyed. There's the sun-glinting silver of the sand. The coarse marram grass bows before the wind to reveal its underskirt of multi-hued flowers. Cowslip, and primrose, periwinkle and daisy. The lambs, that should be too big now not to know better, are crying for their mothers. My hand, overhot, sticky, is enveloped in my father's. And suddenly we're running, his limpy leg dragging. The water is icily splashing, and my satchel is thud, thudding into my back.

"Race you," I shout, and I let go of his hand, and I run out onto the sea-ebb firmness of the wet sand, icy glistening mirroring the sky, and I'm running so fast I might fly.

I fling myself, gasping for breath, through the wind-whipped sand to the calm of a dip in the dunes. He joins me, flushed, breathless, laughing. It's the second time I've beaten him, and I know he's not let me. And we're laughing.

Then we're home, and my mother's scolding the both of us for our wetness, but the laughter is in her eyes. There's tea around the fire, with the flames leaping red and gold crackling up the black crust sculpture of the chimney. Warm.

✦

I looked again out of the window. All of the boats seemed to have gone, and in the darkening the rotating beam from the lighthouse seemed to grow brighter at each turn as it illuminated rhythmically the gentle swell of the waves bereft even of gulls.

And I know that this memory of home is false because incomplete. One-sided. Anyway, it's no longer home.

And the room around me was not my room either. The light as it rotated briefly, rhythmically, illuminated its dusty surfaces, its attempt at homeliness, and the solid planted legs with the hands lying inert in their lap. And it was not the body I knew as mine. The light rotated briefly, mercilessly, illuminating.

I saw, in my mind, for a moment, a scene – it must have been from one of those old war films – as a light rotated from the top of a look-out tower of a prison camp.

And I found myself thinking again of that time in Italy, that summer, when Hartmutt had met me with the fragments of the Wall. My mind – the only part of me that can freely move. Green marble – I'd never been in a bath like it. A mottle of green it was, and the taps gold.

✦

I lay and moved my hand slowly, infinitesimally, up and down so the water shivered and the light on it shimmered as if the marble had liquefied warm around me. Plants in primitive pots trailed and climbed and sprawled, reflected again and again in the mirrored walls so it seemed like a vast garden.

Water embryo warm, moist smells of soil and skin, reflections of reflections, ferns, fronds, uncurling.

The silky warmth of the water caressing my skin.

The dry rough enveloping warmth of Dad's hands.

The small soft vulnerability of Sarah's hand.

Hartmutt's skin, responding.

Dead skin. Cold. Waxy. Unyielding.

Thirteen

And I'm looking at the solid planted legs with the hands lying inert in their lap. I manage to move the right hand slowly so the nail of the thumb digs into the left wrist. I see the nail turn white, sinking into the flesh. The flesh, the nail, feel nothing. I move the nail, see the bloody semi-circle it's made, the skin already bruising around it. And I feel nothing.

I lift the mirror from the table beside me and hold it up to my face, my hands shaking with the weight of it. I hear myself gasp. There's no reflection. I drop the mirror, feel for my face with both of my hands. I can see my hands, feel something stopping them from moving forward.

I hear the splintering of glass as the mirror crashes into the table. I pick it up, turn it over.

I'd been looking into the varnished wooden back of it.

But the feeling's still there. As if I no longer exist.

And I can no longer bear to sit, unmoving, unfeeling, unknowing.

Without really thinking about it I find I'm slithering down out of the chair and I'm rolling over onto my front, and I'm hauling myself, somehow, along the carpet. Digging in toes and knees, elbows, I'm moving forward.

I reach the record player. I lie panting on the floor – breathing in the ancient dust of the carpet, the sweet smell of the decaying floor boards.

When I have the strength to move again I half sit and pull at the pile of records and cassettes on the shelf above my head. A few fall and scatter on the floor and I stir them around looking for something familiar. Like the books in the place they look as if they're a job lot picked up by someone from the University just so there'll be something there. For itinerants like me.

There's a record by the Rolling Stones. I push it to the back of the pile. Then one catches my eye. I pick it up. The cover shows a path, between bushes, narrowing to the horizon, and the backs of two young men in College scarves walking away and turning towards one another, looking behind. Towards me. One of them reminds me of Alasdair. As he used to be. I can't remember if that one is Simon or Garfunkel.

The record is called 'Sounds of Silence'. I get it onto the turntable, and manage to get the player to work. I flop down to lie on the floor beside it.

The first track is called 'Homeward bound', I recognise it when I hear it. Under the guitar melody the drum beat is throbbing and insistent. I turn the volume up. There seems to be a vibration. I turn the bass up. The vibration is stronger. I don't know quite what it is that's vibrating.

Suddenly I hear the word, 'Home'. He keeps saying it, singing it, humming.

'Homeward bound', 'Home'.

My mind drifts off. Switches off.

Then there's a humming, a clicking, and I see the needle arm is gently bouncing against the central spindle through the record. I put the needle back to the beginning, start the turntable revolving again. I try to listen but, somehow, I just can't concentrate and only the same words get through.

Where is my home? With whom?

I don't want to think about it.

I struggle to my elbow to turn the player off, but the track finishes and I flop back. I'm so tired. Somehow I can feel the tiredness right through the body I cannot feel. A heavy, shivery, utter weariness.

The music continues. Loud in Hartmutt's borrowed University flat.

I'm in the middle of the floor and the old floor boards are moving slightly, vibrating with the sound. I can see it. I lie back on the floor and I let the sound flow through me.

Something strange is happening.

I don't want it to happen.

Then the music changes. It's faster with a palpitating drum beat.

There's something strange. At first I don't recognise it. But then I realise it's my body. My body can feel the beat of the drum. The floor boards are reverberating with the beat, shivering its echo into me. I can feel it.

And I can see dust, dust motes hanging just above the carpet, jumping, dancing with the beat. I can smell the sweet smell of decay.

I look towards the chair in the bay of the window. It seems a million miles away.

Then, with a few cords on a guitar again the track changes. A melancholy sound. Gentle voices. The voices shouldn't be gentle.

He's saying something about December. Cold. A window. I don't want to hear it. A shiver shudders through me. Jarring me.

That wasn't my window either.

What wasn't?

December. It was December. There was a lot of snow.

✦

It's dark. I'm sitting on the floor by the window. I move to ease the pain in my legs, but the tape across the starburst in the pane is almost opaque, and I move slightly to the left to avoid it.

The breath-cleared patch in the multi-layered ice patterns is already feathering over, and I breathe on it again, rub at its grittiness with my sleeve. There's maybe a lightening in the sky to the East. It reflects off the ice-patches in the trodden snow.

Somewhere behind me I can hear my mother. She's still breathing.

✦

I become aware of a clicking, a buzzing. The record player. As if of its own accord my hand puts the needle back to the beginning of the last track.

But somehow I can't hear the words. I try to hear the words, but all I can hear is my mother. She's still breathing.

It's buzzing again, and I put it back to the beginning of the track.

And still I cannot get the sound of the breathing out of my mind.

I try to concentrate on the present, on the song. I try to decipher the words.

It says something about being a rock – the song, it says something about being a rock.

Each time the track finishes I struggle up onto my elbow, put the needle back to its beginning, flop back on the floor. I tell myself to stop it – but I keep on doing it. Over and over and over again.

Something's happening. I don't want it to happen.

I've got to find out about being a rock.

So I turn the bass and the volume up as far as they'll go, and I play it again and again. And I hear the words, but they don't seem to be in a language I understand.

And I play it again.

Then, suddenly, I'm quivering.

I try to sit up. Cannot. I prop myself up on my shaking arms and haul myself the short distance to the wall, manage to lean myself up against it.

The quivering becomes juddering and shaking. My barely mobile legs start to jerk convulsively. I put my hands on my knees, try to keep them still. Cannot. And I want so much for it to stop. And that's funny. I've wanted so much to be able to freely move again. Now I can't stop it. And that's so bloody funny. I'm laughing, I'm laughing. I'm crying.

Then I'm lying still on the floor again. I feel so empty. I find I can move my legs a bit by myself. I curl up, knees to chest like a baby. My eyes feel heavy. I close them. Then I realise I know they feel heavy.

Then, like falling off a cliff, I'm asleep.

Fourteen

I awoke to find myself struggling for breath. My face was pressed against a cushion or something, something warm and rhythmically moving. It was dark. I became aware of the sound of breathing, heavy, almost a snore. I moved my head to the side. I could smell Hartmutt's skin, and his aftershave, red wine, rotten floorboards. I moved my right foot, I felt something with it. Hartmutt's calf. There's a duvet over us. His arm around me. I felt my face smiling. I felt myself falling back into sleep.

✦

So, there's the dingy pastel pink of the ceiling, and the wall at the bottom of the bed, and the clock with its second hand jerking round the yellow of its face.

In the distance I could hear the rattle of the drinks trolley, voices, the TV. I knew the window was to the side of me, where I could see out if I just turned my head. But, somehow, I didn't feel the need to. I moved my leg, just a little, just to be sure I still could. Then I must have drifted back into sleep.

✦

"Tea."

"What?"

"I've brought you a cup of tea."

It was Alasdair. He propped me up on the pillows and had the tea down me before I was properly awake.

"Well," he said, "just the one night with Hartmutt, and here we are."

"Och," I said, "he's not as young as he was, he could just manage the five times."

He walked to the window, and looking at the set of his back I knew he'd not say anything else till I did. I sighed, he was so childish at times.

"What's happened Alasdair?" I asked. "I can't remember, just the record. There was a record on the player. I can't remember what it was." His back was now just half turned to me.

"Alasdair, what happened to the rest of the weekend? Do you know?"

"I do indeed," he said, walking back over and sitting in his chair by the bed. "Apparently you started gibbering away in Gàidhlig – you do take after your mother after all – so he brought you back to the hospital." He shifted in his chair. "Not one of his languages."

I could hear the satisfaction in his voice, he looked a lot more relaxed.

"Of course," he said, "being you, by the time they'd dragged me off my golf course you'd decided to go to sleep. Serves me right, I suppose, for taking my bleeper."

"Were you winning?"

"I was winning a game other than golf – with some businessmen who might sponsor that project, you know, that I'm wanting to work on with Alan. Being called away might actually have done us some good. It looked as if I was in demand – he didn't know it was you."

"I'm glad something's going alright, Alasdair," I said, surprised to find I meant it.

"Well," he said, "aren't you going to tell me what happened, what you remembered?"

"What, no Virginia?" I asked.

"She's not into minority languages either."

"We seem to be speaking in the English."

"Strange isn't it," he frowned, "when all was between us as we wanted it to be we always spoke together in Gàidhlig."

"What's that proverb?" I asked, "'Thèid dualchas an aghaidh nan creag, mar a chanas iad' – isn't it? 'heritage will outlast the rocks.'"

"Aye, that's right," he said, "you think now that you have to translate for me."

"Sorry Alasdair."

"No," he said, "no, that's the way of it. There's no need to apologise." He stood and walked over to the window again, and I forgot what it was I'd been going to say.

I could feel his mind moving further from me.

"Alasdair," I said, "do you remember those brochs we went to see, just on the mainland opposite the Isle of Skye? At Glenelg was it? What were they called? Dun Telve and something."

"Dun Troddan," he supplied, grinning, overemphasising the pronunciation 'Doon'.

"Oh, yes that's right," I said, "how could I have forgotten? One of the three or four jokes you've made in the twenty or so years of our marriage. Something about how you saw your role in it."

He grinned again, "Aye, you weren't best pleased with me then either, though for the life of me I couldn't work out why. I so rarely can."

But he walked back over and sat himself down beside me.

I found myself smiling at him, "It was maybe one of those times when the light of science was blinding you to the real."

He snorted, but if he thought of a retort he didn't make it. I wonder if, some time in the future, some professional descendant of Alasdair's will be able to identify people from the same families or marriages by the grooves worn in their brains from such oft repeated phrases.

"Well," he said, "aren't you going to hit me with these ancient rocks?"

"The brochs?" I asked, "We first saw them, didn't we, as we turned the corner of the road, or one of them anyway. The other was round the corner up the hill. You said they looked like beheaded lighthouses. They looked so dark grey and jagged, lichen-spotted against the sky – it was blue for once."

"Age-spots," he said.

But I heard him move and glanced at him to see he was settling as a child for a bedtime story, and I had no idea what the story was.

But I continued anyway.

"They were just beyond the farmhouse, do you remember? and hens were running all around the one lower up the hillside. The red wattles of them were flapping. There were no hens in the higher broch, it wasn't until later I realised why.

"I followed you through the entrance, it was like the sort of tunnel there is in an igloo, do you remember? and stooping to go through it I looked up and saw there were stalactites growing from the top of it. Quite long some of them were, quite thick, and looking as if they might drip at any minute. Still growing. There were no stalagmites, though the slabs that made up the floor of the passage were of the same rock, I wonder why that was?"

He looked as if he was about to tell me, so I hurried on, "Something man had built, about two thousand years ago, wasn't it? Or more – Hartmutt would know – and it was still standing and stalactites were growing from the top of it. The hills and the mountains were just the same as they'd been then, when they were built. I suppose people are too, though there's so much else that's not.

"And I was walking around inside, there was an atmosphere in the both of them. Like there is in a church. But so different one from the other, the hens felt it too, that's why they were just in the one. The lower one was peaceful, like a church, excepting it was warm, but the higher one was cold, really cold and it felt hostile somehow.

"And you were striding around saying how many man-hours it would have taken to build it. How heavy the rocks were – they were huge slabs – how many men it would have taken to lift them.

"After we went back to the car I pretended I wanted to go back and take more photos while you looked at the map, the sun came out just then, do you remember? But really I just wanted to be there by myself, just to feel the feeling of it."

"What are you saying, woman? That my belonging is with the higher broch and your own with the lower?"

I could hear him trying to inject some anger into his voice, but all that came through was the sadness.

"No, Alasdair," I said, "I'm not saying that. I'm not too sure what I am saying. But I'm not saying that."

Is that what I'm saying?

He walked over to the window, and there was silence for a while.

I could feel us both sinking towards a place from where I'd spent too much time and effort climbing.

"Alasdair," I said, "next time you come in, if you don't mind, would you bring in a photo of Sarah? Are there photos of her? I just thought if I could see what she looked like maybe . . ."

He squared his shoulders, came back over and sat down. He took out his wallet. I caught a glimpse of a photo of myself and was so taken aback at that I didn't have a chance to prepare myself. I found myself holding a head and shoulders portrait of a girl of about sixteen or seventeen. I could feel the shivering beginning again deep inside.

"She's got Dad's eyebrows," I said.

"Well, he's no further use for them."

"Alasdair!"

"Sorry, sorry," he said, "I've never introduced an estranged wife to our daughter before. I'm not so sure of the form."

He got up and turned from me, to the window.

"I'm going to get that bloody window bricked up," I shouted at his back.

"Oh, fine," he said, "fine, then maybe it's yourself that'll have to look at things. Brochs. Brochs. Can't you get it into your stupid head, woman, that our daughter is missing?"

"Don't call me 'woman'."

"I'll call you what the hell I please." He sat down glaring at me.

I glared back. "My name is Kate, and I'll thank you to use it. You and the rest of them, I'm sick to death of being called 'love, ' and 'Mrs Err,' and 'my dear.' I'm a person too, you know. My name is Kate."

"Didn't it use to be 'Ceit'?" he asked.

"Oh, don't start that again."

He ran his hand through his hair. He was flushed, blotchy.

"Look," he said, "I'll leave you the photo. Look at it after I've gone."

"Thanks Alasdair."

"There's no need to sound so surprised."

"I do have some idea you know," I told him, "of how it must be for you." I didn't, but perhaps I was just beginning to.

"I'll see you tomorrow," he said. He reached and, for a moment, touched my shoulder, then he hurried out.

I don't know whether I'd felt some of the pressure and warmth of his hand, or imagined it. Or remembered it.

We both deserve better than this.

Fifteen

I looked at her photo, and tried to breathe through the rising panic, tried to feel some connection with the girl – tried to make myself believe she was my daughter. But the clear innocence of the eyes was something that didn't seem to have anything to do with me – though a time there must have been when I'd felt like that – when I'd been like that.

And my thoughts went again to that summer I met Hartmutt.

✦

"No," Dad said, "I don't wish you'd gone home to stay with my mum.

"Now go and get your swimming things before the Embassy ring for me again."

I took his arm and we weaved our way through the streets. People smiled at us but we didn't stop to talk. The sun was rising higher and had burnt all the earlier cloud from the sky – people were clumping in what little shade there was. There was a lot of shouting and laughing, people clapping each other on the back. The Russian ships had moved on from the harbour, and it was a beautiful day.

He'd said he had a meeting that night – I had my suspicions what kind of meeting that was – so he'd be sure to let me go to the barbecue on the beach. Malik'd said he'd see me there.

I had my wooden-soled sandals on, they made a wonderful noise on the cobbles. Flies wafted in the heat and fecund smells rising above the fruit and vegetables piled high on the stalls. The colours were so bright. One of the fat grannies grinned at me and gave me a few of her grapes. They were unwashed, but I ate them.

A boy grabbed my father's arm.

"Marks and Spencers?" he asked, fingering my father's silk shirt.

Pale green it was, beneath his psychedelic waistcoat, and the boy's clothes were threadbare and dull.

We walked on, beyond the town, down to the bay that Dad and I had gone to together so many times before. Not to the more secluded evening beach. It wouldn't be long till evening. I could wear my long fringed skirt, it gave such a nice swirling feeling when we danced, and my white blouse. No, not my white blouse, it'd show up too much if we went for a walk in the trees.

The bay was noisily full of sun-blasted holidaymakers, in and out of the water. On the edge of the beach there was an ice cream stall with a faded striped awning that looked as if it'd been cobbled together out of old deck chairs.

"You go and find a good place," said Dad, "I'll get us ices and join you in a minute."

I laid out our towels and sat down. In the shade the sun was gentle and warm. Soaking into me. There were swifts flying curved-winged amongst the seagulls. The sea was flat and calm, you could see the pebbles, grey and rounded smooth beneath the pale green of the water. The horizon was hazy. A pale greeny blue. No clouds. It was difficult to see where the sea ended and the sky began.

A cliche that was. I'd started to see how many languages I could say it in, when suddenly all the transistors went quiet. I felt goose-pimples breaking out on my arms and legs, I could feel a shivering deep inside. It was as if something like this had happened before, but I couldn't remember what it was.

I looked to the ice cream stall, but there was no sign of Ive or my Dad. Then some of the radios began broadcasting again, in quick panicky bursts through the static. People started shouting and screaming, leaping to their feet and I couldn't make out the words. Some people were giving some of their clothes, belongings, to other people.

I went over to a group where the people weren't crying, asked them what had happened. They were German, and they hushed me as a calmer, more coherent, newsreader began to speak.

The Russians had invaded Czechoslovakia.

The Czechs on the beach, some of them were saying they'd just come to the coast for a couple of days, couldn't go back, only had what they were standing up in. I wanted to say, 'what have clothes got to do with it?', but that seemed to be all they wanted to think about, all they could think about. They seemed sort of glazed somehow. I didn't know what to say, what to do. No one was taking any notice of me anyway.

I went back to where Dad would expect me to be, and just walked up and down, I didn't seem to be able to sit, and eventually he found me. He wasn't wearing his shirt, he had his waistcoat on inside out. Dull grey the lining of it was. He was carrying his holster, he pushed it into the bag beneath our swimming things. I could see the bulge of his gun where he'd pushed it down his sock like a sgian dubh. He was still carrying the ice creams. He didn't seem to know what to do with them. The ice cream had run down his arm in great white streams, the cornets were soggy and transparent. I took them from him, pushed them into a crevice in the rocks.

We went back to the Embassy in Zagreb.

✦

I came back to the present to find the photo still in my hands. I put it in my book just as a nurse entered carrying a tray of food for whatever meal we were up to, and I was glad to concentrate, for the moment, just on that.

Sixteen

The next morning the sun was shining and I awoke with the feeling there was something urgent I should do.

They'd got me up but left me sitting in the wheelchair by the window. Jane'd said she'd be back soon to help me have a wash, but something was happening, I could hear the feet rushing to and fro, a bed being pushed into the side ward beside mine.

I'd managed to give myself a drink of orange from the cup with the spout they'd left by the bed. But I'd poured more down my nightdress than I'd drunk, and my pleasure at managing to give myself any at all had proved more volatile than the juice.

I tried to tell myself how wonderful it was that I could feel the discomfort of the sticky clamminess of the cloth at all, but I was hard to convince.

I wheeled the chair over to the sink and jerked the tap on soaking myself and the floor. I looked to the window in my door for a nurse, to my bell.

I was pushing myself through the door to the showers in my chair, when it occurred to me that both the doors had opened in the direction I was going – they'd be against me on the way back.

Once inside the stall I had to sit and rest, and to shower suddenly seemed a mammoth task. But I got the footrests to the sides of the chair out of the way, and my feet to the floor. I grabbed the handrail and managed to pull myself round and up till my knees were almost straight, but my body was a dead weight, and my arms weren't strong enough and I crumpled to the floor with a great jarring thud.

When I'd recovered and managed to get myself more or less sitting, I pushed the chair away to give me more room, levered myself over to under the shower head and pulled the long cord. I raised my face to the spray. I closed my eyes and I could feel the water, needle sharp spray on my face. I could feel it streaming down me, hair dripping, my nightdress sticking to me, my legs bare on the tiles of the floor. Clean and cool and fresh. The pure gloriousness of being able to feel.

"Mrs MacKinnon, what on earth are you doing?" It was Sister Wilson, not in the best of moods, with Jane looking round her shoulder grinning. The chair was holding the curtain out of position and the floor where they were standing was flooded.

They hauled me into my chair and had me dried, changed, and into my bed in no time.

"Well, alright, dear, but your timing was bad," said Sister, smiling at last, as she hurried out leaving Jane to clear up the debris.

Jane stood looking at me for a while, the wet clothes and towels bundled in her arms. "Well, actually," she said, "your timing was pretty good."

"What is it, Jane?" I asked.

She sat down on the edge of the bed beside me. "Dorothy," she said, "she was ninety three, another of my favourites, she's just died."

She gave a little sob, wiped her mouth with the back of her hand.

"It's so wonderful to see you coming back to life," she said.

She just sat, head bent, and I succeeded, after a great struggle, in getting my hand to her arm. She moved in towards me then and I managed to give her a hug.

After she'd gone I felt myself beginning to drop off to sleep. I could feel the heavy internal swirling of exhaustion. The light-headedness. But I focussed on the other feelings. I felt clean and fresh. I felt I was beginning once more to be myself.

✦

Jane and a porter came in with a wheelchair and I knew I was in for my treat with Virginia.

They got me into the chair and Jane tucked my rug in. She stroked my shoulder, she was still quiet – she'd been crying. I smiled at her, then the porter wheeled me off.

Although she'd rung for me Virginia was still writing notes when they wheeled me in. Or her shopping list maybe.

While I waited I looked around the room, sure it might have been any room in any hospital. And I found myself looking at her.

Her parting wasn't straight, and the lines at the corners of her mouth sloped downwards. She looked up and smiled at me thinly. Just a middle-aged woman she was, tired, with too much to do.

Also, she seemed more sensible when we talked.

◆

I slept again after my lunch. Healing it is they say, but it's something I'm beginning to dread. I used to have nice dreams, some I'd not want to be telling.

But today it was the same images, again and again, though I wasn't always jerked awake at the same point.

◆

There was smoke, choking wreaths of black smoke. Desert, oil rigs. I was wandering alone, bare foot. The sand was burning my feet. I could smell them. Even through the smoke I could smell them.

Faces of the hostages they had taken, the bailed out pilot and the navigator. Beaten. Faces rushing towards me through the smoke, disappearing just before I thought they must hit me.

The tower, the tower computer bombed. And the newsreader's smug voice-over telling us we'd entered the era of clean, impersonal war.

◆

When Hartmutt came striding in I knew straight away that something had happened.

He came and sat on the edge of my bed.

"Hallo, love," he said, "do you fancy a trip out?" He then remembered to bend and kiss me.

"What is it Hartmutt, what's happened?" I asked.

"Sorry, my dear," he said, "they caught me just before I left the site, I seem to have been hurrying all day."

I glanced down at his muddy boots and cords. His nose and ears had a rosy glow, it must be cold.

"Going well is it?" I asked, trying to remember exactly what it was they were trying to achieve.

He sighed, "Yes, I suppose it is, though they're making me feel my age. All this geophysics – machines that can see under the ground – it's brilliant, of course, so much quicker, more efficient. And the computers. But sometimes I feel they're destroying everything I went into Archaeology for. Everything I've built up, got better at over the years."

He strode across to the window.

"I'm being replaced by a bloody hoover," he shouted at his poor reflection.

"Anyway," he turned and strode back, sat down again, "enough of me now. Kate, your mother is asking to see you."

"My mother?"

"Yes." He picked up my hand, I could feel some warmth from it. "They wanted us to go straight away, before she changes her mind. But only if you want to."

"They're trusting us out together again are they?"

"They thought I'd be better than Alasdair because she can't speak to me in Gàidhlig – or at least I couldn't understand her."

"Perhaps they're thinking it'll get her to speak in the English, so they can understand her."

"I don't think so, love. They seem to think she really wants to see you. They think it might help you both. I know last time was awful. You don't have to if you don't want to. I'll bring you back the minute you say."

On the drive there I found myself retelling my encounter with Virginia. Something strange there was about it which I couldn't place at first. Then it struck me that maybe I was telling it close to how it had been. How it had seemed to me, anyway.

So, I found myself back in the conservatory. He left me in my chair by a park bench whilst he went to find her. The old man came out and offered me a cigarette.

They came out hand in hand, my mother looking rather bewildered and anxious. Old.

"Ceiteag, hallo," she said.

"Hallo, Mathair," I said.

She sat herself down on the bench beside me. We seemed, the both of us, to have exhausted our conversational repertoire. She wasn't looking at me.

"I'll go and get myself a coffee," said Hartmutt, and he went.

We sat in silence for a while. I tried to identify some of the plants growing, ill-tended, around us.

After a while I heard her move, and turning saw her with the tears flowing down her cheeks silently crying like a child. I tried to reach out to her, lifted my arms, but I was too far away. I tried to manoeuvre the wheelchair closer, but I couldn't. She noticed my struggling, and seemed to notice, for the first time, the chair.

She wiped her face with her sleeve, asked me what was wrong. I told her that I didn't know. She said she didn't either. Then we talked of home. Of the people we knew, of how it had been. As if then were now. We talked only of that, but we talked. And I found my fluency in the Gàidhlig returning.

✦

When Hartmutt came back for me she stood and wrung her hands, then darted forward and touched my cheek before running out of the door. She'd disappeared by the time we got onto the corridor.

A nurse helped Hartmutt get me into the car, the chair into the boot. He talked to Hartmutt, seemed to be taking ages to go.

When Hartmutt finally got back into the car beside me I reached out for him. I heard him catch his breath, and he gathered me in his arms, supported my head as we kissed. His other hand moved downwards, then stopped.

He sat me back in my seat and put my seat belt on me. There was something closed-looking about his face.

"Hartmutt?" I asked.

"Sorry," he said, "sorry." Not looking at me.

"You mustn't think . . ." I said, "you're under no obligation . . ."

"Kate," he said, "how can you think that?" He glanced at me, then away. "It's just, it seems so wrong, somehow, to touch you when you can't really feel."

He put the key into the ignition, but didn't turn it.

"I don't want it to be like this," he said, through the clenching of his teeth.

I managed to undo my seat-belt then. But it was a brief moment just before, like guilty teenagers, we moved ourselves apart. Still, fortunate it was that it was dark in the car park.

On the way back it was all I could do not to fall asleep in the car. He put me into my chair, I wanted to say something to him, but they'd seen us arrive and came hurrying to help him.

He just bent and kissed my cheek, "goodbye".

They wheeled me back to my bed and got me into it in time for my Horlicks. And for once I was glad of it.

Seventeen

I woke with a start. The moonlight came filtered palely glittering through the thick frost patterns between the curtains where we hadn't pulled them properly across. But all was quiet. Just the sounds of Mum's ragged breathing.

I needed to go to the bathroom. I looked towards the door. It was closed. I watched the door handle. It didn't seem to be moving. I managed to get my legs over the edge of the bed. Holding the table I levered myself up into an almost standing position. Bent over like an old crone I hobbled to the door. I stood holding the door handle listening to my breathing. To the uneven thudding of my heart. I opened the door.

He was there again.

I closed the door and leant against it, a mist I knew wasn't there rising towards me from the floor.

I had to go out. I had to go out. The only alternative was to stay in this room for ever.

He was round the corner. At ninety degrees to me. His side toward me. His back to the wall.

There was room to get past.

I opened the door. He was still there. His dark cloak hooded over the shape of him.

I fast-limped past him and slammed the bathroom door locking it shut behind me. I leant against it, my breath coming in sobs.

Later I knew I would have to go back.

When I opened the bathroom door he was still there. Beyond the bedroom, with his side to it. Facing me now. The long hood drooping forward. His head bent. His arms folded, their hands up the opposite sleeves. His dark cloak hooded over the shape of him.

I couldn't run. Slowly I walked towards him. Towards the door of the bedroom. Keeping an eye on him. Keeping a hand on the wall.

I saw his head beginning to move just as I began to get close to the door. I stopped. I stood and watched as he lifted his head. He lifted his head and looked full at me.

Looked at me with his eyes black holes of seeing in the skull that was all of his face.

Eighteen

I slept – on and off – all day, despite the fear that the nightmare would return. So when the time for Alasdair to come approached I wasn't feeling as tired as usual – as has got to be usual – so I asked them to help me to sit in the chair. Jane and Ellen it was – my favourite combination of nurses, though maybe some of their colleagues wouldn't have understood just why.

They gave me a quick wash, just the bits that showed. Jane gave me a squirt of her perfume – just the one – for it was Alasdair that was coming not Hartmutt.

"You've decided how my future's to be, have you, Jane?" I was laughing, though not so long since I'd have been annoyed.

"She's a romantic," said Ellen, "she sees you going hand in hand into the sunset with the bearded one."

"'The bearded one', now there's a name I hadn't thought of for him."

"I'm sorry, Mrs MacKinnon, I didn't mean to be rude."

"No, no, it's alright, Ellen, I'm not offended, I don't know how you remember all the names of your patients, never mind their visitors."

"I've got them all written down, with the room numbers," she said, "or the bed numbers in the ward." She pulled a used envelope out of her pocket and showed me the list scribbled on the back of it. I caught a glimpse of my name but she'd shoved the list back into her pocket before I managed to read the comment scrawled beside it.

"A lot of rooms," I said, "I suppose it'd be easier for you if we were all in the ward."

"No," Jane said, "I like the rooms, it's nice not to be watched all the time."

"I like the rooms best too," said Ellen, "it's like that game, you know, on the telly – not the Krypton factor, the other one – a different challenge behind every door."

"The Crystal cave, no, maze," said Jane.

"That's the one," said Ellen.

I'd never seen it.

They manoeuvred me into the chair and when we'd all got our breaths back they began to tidy me up. The back of my hair was tangled where it'd rubbed on the pillow. I must have been moving again, in my sleep.

Is a challenge how I want people to see me? Is that really what I've become?

"I haven't heard about Paul for a while, Jane," I said, "is everything alright."

"Well, actually," she said, "he's asked me to move in with him." She continued to brush my hair though it was no longer pulling. I tried to keep my concentration on her, I'd always liked having my hair brushed, and to be able to feel it happening was so good.

"I don't know what to do," she said.

"No," I said, "it's always easier knowing what other people should do, isn't it? So hard for yourself."

"I just want things to go on being as they are," she sounded very sure of that. "But Paul won't have that."

"No," I said, "relationships do have a habit of growing and changing whether we want them to or not. Or shrinking and changing. We want them to be something they're not."

But then, thankfully, Nurse Armstrong put her head round the door to tell them Alasdair was waiting to see me, and they left.

Me, the expert on relationships.

He seemed pleased with himself for once. He told me that Alan and he'd raised a sponsorship, at last, for their project – though it'd mean moving, in the new year, to a Hospital in Glasgow. I found I was genuinely pleased for him.

But then he waffled on for ages about the arrangements he was planning for my care when I left the Hospital. I was aware of the general drift though the details went by me.

"Kate," he shouted, glaring at me, "can't you at least have the courtesy to listen to me?"

"Alasdair," I said, "I haven't even decided yet what I want to do when I leave here."

"Oh, for God's sake," he said, "do you think you can lie here dreaming for ever? There are people, you know, who are actually sick, who could maybe use your bed."

"They say it'll be a couple of weeks yet before they'll be happy to let me go."

"I don't see why it needs to be that long – but we've got to make plans now anyway." He let out a long deep breath, managed something approaching a smile.

"Come on," he said more quietly, "what's her name? That woman – you know. Let down your hair," he frowned towards the window.

And I had a picture of myself, Rapunzel, and himself reaching up towards me. Traction alopecia is it?

But I was smiling, I could feel the smile on my face – and the sadness inside.

I looked out of the window at the leaves now fully opened on my tree. The sky was cloudless and blue.

I looked back at him, and I saw the pale thinnings of his formerly thick and fiery hair. He looked tense, too, about the muscles of his jaw.

"Alasdair," I said, "I want a divorce." I heard myself saying the words, though I'd not planned to say them.

There was a long silence then he said, "Kate, this isn't the time to make decisions like that. Any decisions." He was upset.

"It's not a decision," I told him, "it's an acceptance of the way things are, the way they've been for a long time. Far, far too long. For both of us."

"No," he said, "this isn't the right time to discuss things like that."

"There's never a right time for many things," I said, "but that doesn't stop them happening."

He walked over to the window.

"Alasdair," I said.

"No," he said, "I'll not discuss it with you now. When you remember it could change everything."

"But . . ."

"No," he said, "I've told you, I'll not discuss it with you now. Not until you're better. Not until we know what's happened."

"Alasdair, that time may never come."

"Yes, it will. Yes it will. All you've got to do is remember."

I moved my hand, found the bell tucked underneath my pillow. They'd put it at the wrong angle, but I managed to manoeuvre it round and press it.

"I suppose you want Hartmutt to marry you at last. He does seem to go for the halt and the lame – like some sort of post-feminist Jane Eyre," he said.

The thought to point out who that would make him came to me – but I didn't say it. The anger I'd got used to calling on for protection was no longer there, it no longer seemed relevant somehow.

Ellen came, and I got her to take me to the toilet. I was so tired, but it was Ellen, and she made no comment when I asked her just to leave me in my wheelchair for a while. She locked the door behind us, and lit a cigarette, opening the window so she could blow the smoke out to disperse into the chill of the air. I was shivering.

Why can't he just let me go?

There must have been a better way of dealing with it than that.

I've not hidden in the toilets since school.

"Mum," said Sarah, "you're useless – being frightened of thunder at your age." She was grinning, glad to be one up on me, though I could see her fear too – in her eyes.

"Sarah," I said, "come away from that window."

I was jerked back to the present by a knock at my door.

"Hallo, bearded one," I said, as the door opened and Hartmutt's head appeared around it, "come and sit down." Glad I was to see him.

He grinned and, for once, did as he was told. "What did you call me?" he asked.

"Oh," I said, "it's just the girls – they're making up all sorts of things. I expect you do need something of a fantasy-life, working in a place like this."

"Yes." He paused. "Jane told me that you'd asked Alasdair for a divorce – very indiscreet of her – though I'm sure she means well."

I smiled at him, though our eyes didn't quite meet. "She sees us spending our twilight years together," I told him.

He was silent for a while, I could hear the slight rasp of his breathing. At his age he shouldn't be so much out of doors.

"I was hoping," he cleared his throat, "I was hoping that the twilight years were soon to be over, for both of us."

He reached for my hand, "In fact, I'm seriously thinking of buying a couple of pairs of sunglasses. Not necessarily a matching pair of pairs, I'm not Jane. Though I'm . . ."

He let go of my hand, sat up straighter, sighed. "It's far too soon for you to be thinking of the future. Except the practicalities of the immediate future. No need to think about the future now."

"I've been thinking what I could do now," I said, "with my linguistics, it wouldn't matter for that if I couldn't walk properly – though I don't believe yet that I shan't walk properly again – but I'd prefer to be mostly in one place now anyway. I've enjoyed so much working for TEFL, and interpreting for your conferences and Dad's, and all the books and things I've translated. It made sense. And it was mostly fun. But there's nothing to fit round now. I want to do something more in one piece. More substantial."

He smiled, "Good, and you know I'll help you if I can – when the time comes."

He touched my arm. "Alasdair phoned me late last night," he said, "we discussed practicalities then too, though he didn't mention your earlier conversation. He suggests that you go and live in your old house for now – when you come out I mean – he'll continue to stay in the Doctors' Residence."

He stretched his legs out in front of himself again. "I've still another eight or nine months here, I can help you," he said. "I'm doing a little re-thinking of my own. You'll be alright. Just till we all know what we're doing. There's your Mum too, of course. You can get home helps and things."

He smiled at me again, "You perhaps need to begin to think about it anyway."

"Yes," I said, "I will. When are you coming in again?"

He stood up slowly.

"No," I said, "I didn't mean – I mean, I do want to know when you're coming again, know how long there is to think, not that I'm short of time to think. But I don't want you to go – not unless you want to, of course. You must be very busy."

He sat down again, though on the edge of the seat just. "You don't have to decide by the next time I come," he said. "They're not planning to throw you out just yet. The day after tomorrow I think I should be able to make it."

"Hartmutt," I asked, "do you want to tell me? Do you remember . . . ? What do you remember of Sarah?"

"Sarah – a lovely girl," he smiled and settled himself back into his seat, relaxing.

"I just thought," I said, "if I had a clearer picture, it might help me remember what's happened."

"Kate," he said, "it's alright. It's a good idea.

"The time I remember her best is that time in Italy. You know, when I was at the conference in Assisi and went on to see that Franciscan Monastery Domenico was restoring. August." He smiled at me, "You came to meet me, en route to some job in Istambul."

"Did he ever manage to get it finished? Domenico."

"Yes. He ground to a halt for a while, of course, lack of funds. He came back to me on it, I managed to help him get a grant – the floors of the underground passage were of great interest, they were much earlier. Now there are droves of tourists, St Francis key rings and all. And those curious T-shaped crosses. It was a year or so ago I last saw him. He's getting old.

"90 or 91 it would be, just after the Berlin Wall came down – I can never remember when that was."

"90," I said.

"Sarah was ten, or eleven – was she?" he asked.

"She'd be eleven," I said. She hadn't been there.

"Yes," he went on, "that was a good couple of weeks. Though the outcome might have been very different."

He looked at me, but I just smiled – what else could I do? The past is in the past, unchangeable.

"Yes," he said, "and that bloody bathroom – do you remember it? All mirrors, and trailing plants that made a grab for bits of you as you got out of the bath. A marble bath that took all the heat out of the water. Though the spiders liked it."

He reached for my hand and kissed it. We were silent for a while.

"That was the real start of her interest in Archaeology – I'd never got you to come to any of my digs on your own."

"And all the times we had tea in tea rooms afterwards. Assorted sandwiches and scones with mud still under our nails."

"Or brewing up on the camping gaz, Sarah ordering me where to sit. Though I must say that I've been used for many worse things than a windshield."

"Pretty child, so full of life and curiosity. That long blonde hair that got so tangled, and muddy – she wouldn't tie it back. And her 501's. She had to explain their importance to me. As if the sheep were fashion-conscious," he paused, smiling.

"Pity you and Marie were never able to have children," I said.

"I used to regret it so much," he said, "especially soon after she died. I'm just so glad now to have had her for as long as I did. I thought I'd never get over it. But the horror of those last months has faded somehow, and I can remember again the good times we shared. Made. Thirteen years. I was so angry it had been cut short. But it might have changed anyway. I've seen it happen so often, too often, amongst my friends, people I care for."

"Did you know Alasdair grumbled at your wedding that all the speeches were in German?" We smiled at one another. "It was the first time he'd been out of Britain," I said.

"You were both so young when you married, too young," he said. I nodded.

"There was something about Sarah sometimes," he said, "and I saw in her how you must have been. Perhaps you never were. Something of Alasdair in her too. Your Mother."

After he'd gone I reached for my book. Opened it where I'd put her photo under the plastic dust cover.

Oh Sarah, what are you thinking, feeling? Are you somewhere frightened, alone? Hurt?

We wouldn't have left you alone. Couldn't.

Sarah?

"Reading again?" asked Ellen, dumping a cup of Horlicks on my bed-side table. "You'll strain your eyes in this half-light."

She put the light on as she left the room, but she was in too much of a hurry to turn and see my face.

Nineteen

That night I drifted in and out of sleep, waking suddenly again and again the edges of dreams receding, till finally I was so tired I stayed with the dream.

✦

An old man helped me down onto the deck. I didn't think I was going to be able to make it, didn't think my legs could bend or stretch so far. The sea churned and surged, oily-foamed, in the widening and narrowing gap between the boat and the concrete of the quay, the cracked tyre creaked with the changing of the pressures on it. I was afraid that my leg might get stuck in the gap.

In the end he just gave my arm a tug and I landed heavily, half against him. He gave me a gap-toothed grin, then I dumped my bag on the deck and between us we hauled Mum aboard just as they cast off. I grabbed the rail and Mum as the boat rocked and juddered and the engine spurted smudges of oil-laden smoke into the heavy greyness of the sky. I hardly had time to catch my breath and nod my thanks at the man before we started to chug from the dock.

I looked for a better place, then picked up the bag, and Mum and I lurched across the deck towards it between the people and their belongings. There was a goat sitting on the deck attached to the side of the boat by some rope. There were a few old men huddled muttering together, their bags of carvings hanging lumpily from their shoulders.

We lowered ourselves to the wet deck close to the pole in its centre. We sailed from the harbour straight into the wind. We clung to each other, we were as far as we could get from the icy needles of foam that were scooped up to the wind by our dipping bow. But they still reached us.

Cold the sea looked. Rough.

The boat yawed and creaked and my mind blanked into the rhythm of it.

When first we saw land it was difficult to believe it was real, though there were seagulls in plenty wheeling and crying to tell us it was so. I had to struggle to try to remember where it might be.

Then I saw the tall thin Barbers poles on the jetties, and the arches and bridges. Venice.

The boat tied up to the sloping jetty and they helped us ashore. They hadn't stopped quite far enough in and the water as we landed slopped over our feet. The planks were slippy with ice.

Mum and I just stood for a while, as people scurried away. Soon there were just the two of us. I couldn't think what it was we were supposed to do.

I looked at my watch.

Different time-zone, we must change the time we have an hour. Forward or back? I don't know.

Mum was shivering and shuddering – singing quietly to herself – so I started to walk, pulling her along roughly till she got going.

We got to a square that looked familiar. The grey flagstones of the square were dull, and the white line patterns of the paler flags seemed to shimmer in the fading light.

We stood for a while. Then I noticed we were shaking. I suppose it must have been cold. We started to move again, first in one direction, then in another. The streets were like canyons, and the uneven pavements were icy and treacherous.

The canals were narrow, and odd pieces of washing strung abandoned across them creaked stiffly in the wind.

'Come on,' I told myself, 'you've got to get us there.' I still wasn't sure where it was we were going, but, somehow, I knew I'd recognise it when we got there.

Arches and bridges. Canals and a lowering sky.

Then, suddenly, a building I knew.

I kept my finger on the bell till one of the shutters was angrily thrust open.

Then, there was the soft padding of feet on the stair. And the door opening.

Smells of garlic and turpentine.

Roberto.

✦

In the morning I found it difficult to throw the dream off. The feeling of it. Even when Jane was washing me. She just smiled at me, for once, and got on with her job.

"Jane," I said, "my injuries can't be entirely real, can they, or I wouldn't have been able to get back to Roberto's with Mum."

"Oh, is that what it is?" she asked.

She put the flannel down and sat on the bed beside me.

"Where ever your injuries are based, so to speak, they are real – you mustn't think they're not. The mind is as real as the body, you know. Anyway we don't know it is your mind."

I managed to grab the edge of the sheet and dry my cheek with it. I felt cold somehow.

"Anyway," Jane went on, "we don't know how far you had to go, you could have been just round the corner from Roberto. And people are capable of doing extra-ordinary things if they need to enough. I've seen some of that here, you know, as well as people that give up for no reason that you can see at all.

"People walk across fields with one amputated arm tucked under the other, and don't keel over till they reach help. I've seen it, honest."

She looked over her shoulder to see who was walking by in the corridor – but it was just another student nurse.

"There was a farmer a few weeks ago," she said, leaning closer to me, "he dangled into his combine harvester – they do quite often, it jams and they get off to free it without turning it off, and of course it starts again. Anyway, this man, he was dead lucky, it was a clean cut, and he thought to pick it up. We've got good micro-surgeons here, micro for the capillaries and things, I mean, not for him – he was average – most men are, aren't they – and fortunately he was a common blood group, but he was a bachelor, and they wanted to know if they'd done a good job."

She picked up the flannel again and rinsed it in the bowl of soapy water.

"So," she said, "they told him the best place to go for women, you know they come here for health checks. I bet you didn't know you could get advice like that on the NHS."

She resumed my wash and continued to chat, and though I was touched she so obviously wanted to make me feel better, I just wanted, more than anything, for her to shut up.

I was very glad when Hartmutt came and we set off to see Mum once more. I'd forgotten she'd been getting me ready for that.

The journey seemed familiar this time, though short. But when we got to the car park, after he'd turned the engine off, he just sat with his hands on the wheel, looking out of the non-too clean windscreen at the red brick wall ahead.

"Are you alright, Hartmutt?" I asked eventually.

He turned and smiled at me. "Yes love, fine," he said. "It's just, I wanted to tell you, I've been thinking."

"Yes," I said.

"I've decided," he said, "not to wait for the new technology to hoover me up, you know?"

"Yes," I said, smiling, "I remember."

"It would be ridiculous, at this stage of my career, to try to get into it. So I've decided not to. I don't know yet what I will do. Plenty of choice. Something more academic, perhaps, I don't know. It'll need some thinking about."

"That must've been a hard decision, Hartmutt," I said, "you've always loved the field work. But I'm sure you're right."

He smiled at me, "I don't know where it'll be either."

"That's okay, Hartmutt," I said.

When we got to the conservatory I got him to help me to stand, I walked the couple of steps to the park bench and sat myself down there. He reached to my chair for my rug.

"Hartmutt," I said, "I'm not an invalid."

He smiled, "Well, I suppose it is quite warm in here."

He left me to go in search of Mum.

She looked better, somehow. Her hair seemed not so uncared-for, her dress was on straight. She was standing straighter too.

Hartmutt left us as soon as he saw we'd settled. I wonder what he does to amuse himself while we're here.

We talked as before of home, but somehow, now, I knew that she knew it was in the past. And to me it seemed very distant, though I was speaking the language like a native.

She seemed to see me when she looked at me. She smiled at me now and again, patted my hand. She looked again like my Mum, so I said to her – still in the Gàidhlig – "Mum, where's Sarah?"

She looked at me as if completely uncomprehending. There was a long silence. She started twisting the hem of her dress.

I got my hands to her shoulders, tried to shake her. I wanted to shake her. "Mum," I shouted, "Mum, what's happened to Sarah?"

She took my hands and held them. Then looking at me she said – in the English – "Who's Sarah?"

We were sitting in silence when Hartmutt came back and rescued me safe to my bed.

Twenty

I lay for a while with my mother's arm flung across my shoulder. She was snoring quite loudly, though she'd be sure to deny that if I were ever to mention it to her. Too much to drink the night before. My own head felt a little muzzy and my mouth was dry. I turned my head and looked over the edge of the bed. On her mattress on the floor Sarah was curled up on her side with her hair streaming red gold over the pillow above her. She looked so young.

I carefully eased my mother's arm from around me and managed to get my feet to the floor between the bed and Sarah. She stirred and gave a little sigh as I stepped over her, but she didn't wake.

I made my way across the vast studio towards the kitchen. In the early morning light the canvases cast shadows against the walls. The light was very bright and clear – cold. So different from the place where I'd first met Roberto. That's success for you. But the smells were the same. Garlic and turpentine. I breathed in deeply. I'd been uncertain about coming, but now I was sorry it was time to be leaving.

I ran the tap in the kitchen until the water was cool. I lifted the blind, but across the canal and the inevitable washing the window opposite seemed too close, and I lowered it again. I wandered back with my water into the studio, went to look again at the portrait on his easel. So different from the picture he'd done of Mum all those years ago. Funny, I'd have thought he'd have wanted to paint Sarah.

I heard the soft padding of feet, and turning saw Roberto coming towards me, barefoot, bare-legged in a blue and white striped nightshirt. He looked relaxed and sleepy, and his white curls were dishevelled around the stubble of his jowls. He put his arm around my shoulders.

"Quite a woman, huh?" he said.

We stood together looking at her, and, seeing through his eyes, I saw she was. I looked at him smiling so gently at the painted wrinkles and flaws that I usually filtered out, and the light that was her that I somehow didn't really see either, and I finally realised what it was that she saw in him.

"I'm so glad we came, Roberto."

He laughed. "I am too. And that Sarah, she's good, better than Anna, though don't tell either of them I said so."

"Don't worry," I said, "I won't. Strange how these things seem, so often, to miss a generation."

"Oh, you have your compensations," he said.

"You didn't think that when first we met. God, I must have been obnoxious."

He laughed again, and gave me a hug.

Then Sarah got up and we were into breakfast, and suddenly we were at the time to leave.

✦

"Come on, Kate, wake up now," Jane had her hand on my shoulder, "time for me to give you a wash and brush up for your visit to your favourite person."

I looked at her uncertain for a moment which was the reality.

Then, "Virginia?" I asked, in mock horror, even managing to make the fingers of my right hand shake.

"None other," she replied, making the sign of the cross with her fingers like you do to ward off the vampires.

Then, for a moment, our eyes met – so she sat herself down on the edge of the bed, smiling. "In that case I'll just give your hair a quick brush," she said. "Oh I forgot, they rang this morning, from St Mary's, they said to tell you that your mother has been painting. A picture of some mountains, and mist and things."

She started then to brush my hair, she hummed a little whilst she was doing it. I could feel the pulling of it, and it was still so strange and wonderful just to be able to feel it that I was glad of her roughness.

"Your hair's improving," she said, standing back to admire her handiwork, "it's getting a shine back to it."

"Good," I said. "You seem a lot happier this morning, Jane, has something happened?"

"Yes," she said. "I told Paul I'm not going to live with him. Silly really – if I needed to think about it, it couldn't have been the right thing could it?"

I smiled at her, "How did Paul take it?"

"Amazing. He said if it wasn't right for me, it couldn't be right for him. There's hope for us yet."

✦

"It's really quite simple," I said.

Virginia sat back in her chair and steepled her fingers, waiting for me to go on.

"Things just seemed to come together, really."

She made the sort of non-committal noise she was so good at.

"Mum had been wanting to go back and see Roberto for ages," I continued, "he's her Italian painter friend she met at an exhibition in the sixties."

She nodded.

"And there were all Dad's papers and things to sort out, and everything. We'd never even been to his grave – you can't say goodbye properly, can you? unless you've seen the grave. Mum wanted to do that too. So did I."

She dropped her hands to her lap.

"Not a choice, anyway, all his papers and things had to be attended to sooner or later," I said. "That area – there was never going to be an ideal time to go. And then Sarah came up with this idea – and it was the obvious thing to do, a good thing to do. That's how it seemed at the time.

"And there really are so few people who speak the language.

"And a chance for the three of us to be together, we so rarely are."

I glanced at her but she just nodded. One of her talents – she could out-silence the statue of a deaf-mute.

"We knew he'd never understand – Alasdair – that was the only problem."

I turned and looked out of her window. It had taken me several sessions to work out that her office was directly under my room. I could see now only the rather battered trunk of the tree that through my window was a mass of swaying branches wreathed with pale delicate leaves opening into new life. Bet she wouldn't want to explain the significance of that to me.

"So in the end we just decided to go ahead anyway." I moved my head slightly.

"We agreed we'd tell him after," I said.

I found myself giggling. "We didn't say how long after," I managed to get out before the giggles overtook me. I got the hiccups then, and eventually she got up and brought a glass of water, helped me sip it till they quietened. My eyes were watering.

She went and sat down again and folded her hands in her lap and waited for me to go on. I'd always been able to sit in the silence on my own, it was a great luxury that came far too infrequently, but with her, somehow, it was impossible.

"We'd agreed to tell him when it was all over, when he couldn't come up with all the things that could go wrong. Dampen it down as he did so often with things that people wanted to do. That they were enthusiastic about.

"He'd never have understood.

"Sarah had heard about it through someone she met at the Leisure Centre, a boy she sometimes meets when she goes swimming there. I don't think there's anything in it. They just have a coffee and a chat afterwards. He races, she says he's given her some tips – though she only does it for the pleasure of it. And to get fit.

"She doesn't eat enough.

"Mum told her she put more nourishment on her hair than she did in her stomach. I don't remember either of my grans. Well, just my Father's mother a little when I was small. An old lady dressed in black. Fierce she was.

"Anyway he said he was going with his dad and a couple of other people, and he put us in touch with the organiser.

"And sure enough they did need an interpreter, and it seemed such a good thing to do. To help. I've interpreted so often at talks in trouble spots. I suppose I thought it would be like that somehow. We didn't know the first thing about it. None of us do.

"They'd collected a whole lorry-load of stuff – they'd advertised for donations in the local paper. They were driving the lorry there.

"So, anyway, that's what we arranged. We'd tell Alasdair and people we were going to stay with Roberto for a fortnight. We'd stay with him a week, meet up with the lorry at the UNPROFOR post at Trieste – they had machinery and medical supplies, blankets to unload – then we'd go with them whilst they gave out the Christmas parcels, help them with that. And with translation, whatever was needed – just a few days – then they'd drop us back at Trieste. They were leaving the lorry there, giving it to them.

"And then we'd make our own way to Dad's – there was peace then, it was never much in the war zone anyway – just out beyond Zagreb. I checked. The trains were still running. Sometimes there were three a day, sometimes just the one – but they were still running. So it was bound to be alright. We'd stay there a couple of days, sort things out. Then we'd come back home."

I looked out of the window again. The grass needed cutting.

"I don't know what happened then.

"I've thought of so many possibilities.

"I don't know.

"I don't know. She's younger than us, maybe she decided to stay there and do something to help. What's age got to do with it? In Trieste – or somewhere.

"Ever since I was eleven I've travelled alone across the world to Embassies to spend the summer holidays with Dad. There were three of us. He was posted to worse places than that.

"I can't remember. She was with us when we got back to the UNPROFOR place. I remember that. I know that.

"No, I'm not getting confused with the first time we were there.

"She's alright. She's alright I tell you."

Twenty One

I've got to the stage now when I'm no longer fighting the oncoming of sleep. Where not knowing seems worse than knowing – though that's maybe only because I don't know.

That night I lay long in the space between waking and sleeping. Some night bird was singing alone and clear in the dark. I lay and listened and wasn't aware of the drift into sleep – or whatever it was.

✦

We boarded the train at Trieste.

We rattled on through the countryside with the carriage nearly to ourselves. Just an old woman, enveloped in black, sat near the door with her rosary, or mala, mouthing words in silence. And sitting there, watching the both of them sleeping, my daughter's head on my mother's shoulder, was the first time that I'd really thought much about what we'd agreed to do. It had all been arranged so much on the spur of the moment. It had all seemed to fit together so well – almost as if it'd been meant, somehow.

And she'd been so enthusiastic. About her idea. Thinking we should get involved, make a difference in the world. We'd thought that too, at her age.

All the information we're bombarded with – till we all know far too little about far too much – and the unthinkable becomes normal.

I kept trying to think of what we'd just left, of how I'd been. Of how I wish I had been. But my mind wouldn't stay on the thoughts.

So then it was, looking out of the window at the countryside speeding past, that I got to thinking of Alasdair. Thinking of why it'd become impossible to tell him we what we were planning to do. Too many other things too, untold, unshared, unfaced.

We'd had a good relationship once.

Christmas we'll have together, tell him all about our journey. Then I'll do something about it. Himself and me.

✦

Dad's flat was just as it always had been – if you didn't look out of the windows. Only it was dusty, and cobwebby and cold. It was so familiar to me it was difficult to really believe that neither Mum nor Sarah had ever been there. But there was something unfamiliar about it too. I'd never been there without Dad.

I was standing, just looking round, breathing in the dank, musty, smell – trying to tell myself this was real – when Sarah started scrabbling in her bag at my feet.

"Ohh," she said.

"What is it, love?" I asked.

"They're all crumpled," she said. There were tears in her eyes, she was exhausted.

"It's alright," said Mum, "she won't mind that." She was smiling.

"Come on now, you two, what's all this?" I asked.

Sarah stood and put into my arms the most ill-wrapped bunch of half-dead chrysanthemums I'd ever seen.

"I thought you'd be sad . . . coming here," she said.

I didn't know whether to laugh or cry. They'd probably originally been yellow, or pink.

"Where ever did you find these?" I asked.

"Trieste," she said.

"Oh, Sarah," I said, "they're the most beautiful present I've ever had. Thank you."

We searched, but all we could find to put them in was an empty whisky bottle. No water. We had to get out the camping gaz and melt some snow for them. We gave them pride of place on the mantle.

It was very cold, there were no lights. We found some bedding and although it felt damp we made up the beds and just tumbled, fully dressed, into them. Sarah took the futon in the living room. It wasn't much better than the mattress at Roberto's.

We were all up early. Sarah made us some tea on the camping gaz and we all drank it huddled in blankets sitting on the floor – we left the gaz on low. It was so quiet and peaceful.

We pulled the rosewood panel away from the front of the fireplace and I went out to the woods at the back to see if I could find anything else that we'd be able to get dry enough to burn.

I remember as a child, walking to home, always picking up cones and wind-fallen twigs to go on the Rayburn. Dad and I had gone collecting together, sometimes, when Mum was painting and the pot had a long time yet on the stove till we could sit to eat. He knew where the otters lived in the bank, and sometimes – around dusk – we'd see them.

A great quietness there was in the woods. The bracken had all been snapped off just above the height of the snow. Long since. The stumps of the stems were blackened with frozen ooze. The trees were scabbily-barked and all the branches within possible reach had been broken off – torn off, still green, most of them, taking with them great flays of trunk. There were no traces of small animals, no birds.

I followed the path to make sure I could still find the way to the cemetery – we'd agreed we'd all go together after we'd sorted his papers and things out – but the way was well worn. Walking between the graves I was aware of the openness of the ground, the hills overlooking. I could feel the exposure of my back, dark-coated against the blue-white glare of the snow. I met no one.

But, sitting on my heels, probably just outside the low, snow-buried walls around his plot, reading his name and dates, though it was a shock, still, to see them, I knew he wasn't there. It was in me he was – more than I'd known – and I felt a kinship with him then in the new-found knowledge of our shared weakness more than I'd ever felt in our shared strengths, perhaps a greater understanding too.

I stood looking at his grave. Then I remembered he was in Sarah too, and in the memories of all who had known him.

Walking back through the woods I was aware of the bracken, and the trees, but mostly I was aware of the sky.

They'd found his old psychedelic waistcoat scrunched up at the back of a drawer – wrapped around his gun – it was difficult to believe he'd ever worn it. Sarah'd put it on over her two jumpers, the mirrors of it were glinting, you could see how it'd been folded, the colours of the embroidery less faded on the front than on the back.

They were sitting on the floor, leaning heads together, their breath white plumes in the still air. There were papers, and boxes, cards, in a semi-circle spread before them. They'd obviously not done much, got caught up looking at an old photo album, letters.

Everything had a strange feel to it, as if we were actors just pretending, and the world around us was not quite real.

I caught a glimpse of a photo of myself with Dad, standing by some fine blossoming mimosa. I looked about Sarah's age.

"Yes," said Sarah, catching me looking, "I have seen it, Mum. And you grumble at me for the way I look sometimes when I go out. Your hair's nearly as long as your skirt."

But it's not the vast expanse of leg I'm looking at, it's my hand in Dad's.

And the sun is warm to the top of my head. The sea is cold to my feet, surging up to my knees. Foaming. The sand, as I step, grittily squidges up between my toes, round the edges of my feet, sinking me into it.

"Race you," I shout, and I let go of his hand.

I'm on the wet sand. And the sand's icy, glistening, mirroring the sky.

Then we're home. Tea around the fire, with the flames leaping red and gold crackling up the black crust sculpture of the chimney.

Warm.

And that's where we should be now, and Alasdair with us, in that kitchen that Sarah's never known.

✦

In the afternoon we went together to his grave. It seemed different now we were together, and somehow, just those few minutes there made his passing seem final – something that none of our grieving had done.

They'd found a bottle of whisky in his flat and on our return there we sat, red of nose and ear, round the camping gaz, with his chunky

Bohemian red and gold wine glasses, well filled, slippily clutched in our gloves.

"Slàinte mhath!" said Sarah, raising her glass. The only Gàidhlig she knows.

Mum and I replied, then we sat just quiet, the three of us. I could feel the warmth of the spirit spreading through me. I looked around his flat. It was no longer the place I'd known. The gaz hissed, its small even flames imparting their smell to the air. Quiet it was.

Sarah topped up our glasses, straightened her legs. "Why did Grandad stay when the war was on?" she asked. "He'd already retired, he didn't have to go back and work with them." She pushed her hair back from off her face, they both needed washing, "They knew he had shell shock before. They shouldn't have let him. He should have come home."

"Well it was his home wasn't it?" said Mum. "He'd made it his home. Anyway he was a brave man."

She took a sip of her whisky, smiled at Sarah, "'Lack of moral fibre' they called it then. Knowing him I came to see that only those who've really known fear, faced it, can be truly brave. I'm proud I've known him."

Mum smiled at me, "I know that sounds trite."

I shook my head, but she continued as if I hadn't.

"It's the simple truth, however. I don't know how else to say it." She swirled the whisky round in her glass. "I had such mixed feelings when he wanted to stay on Eilean a' Goath, when life seemed just to be beginning. Our plans had been so different. But, the fact is, I've had the best of both worlds.

"It had its problems, any way of life does, and sure if we'd stayed there much longer we'd all have suffocated . . ."

She bent her knees up, put her arms round, hugging them.

"But I couldn't go on living with him – he was so driven to prove himself courageous, that too much else got thrust aside. He always was – brave, I mean – and he spent his life working with others who, some of them, needed to prove themselves human."

She took a sip of her drink. "Not what we planned. If he'd been just a few months younger he'd have missed the War completely. Life can change in a moment."

"Yes, Mum," I said, "but it can change for the better too."

"It's like Yugoslavia, really, isn't it?" asked Sarah.

"Yugoslavia?" I asked her.

"Yes," she said, looking from me to Mum, then out of the window. Her eyes were so like her father's.

"I don't understand the Communists," she said, "though we've done them in school. They made the Berliners stay apart, built a wall, then when they'd become separate, too different for it to work, they made them come together again."

She paused, frowning, then continued, "And the Yugoslavs they made stay together too long, till they'd intermarried and mixed, and then they forced them apart, when you could no longer see the joins. I don't understand politics, really, perhaps I will when I'm older."

"Perhaps I will when I'm older," said Mum.

"I know that's naive," said Sarah, "there's no need to pretend you're not smiling, but then so too – even more so – are most of the people involved."

"Yes," said Mum.

"It seems to me," I said, "that the greatest tragedy is pretending there's a norm to which we should all aspire – that it's a simple question.

"And that prejudice is a choice, not a gut reaction."

I glanced at Mum, "We want people to be something they're not."

We were quiet for a while, just listening to the wind as it found, worried at, the delapidations of the flat, outside. In the distance there was intermittent rumbling – thunder perhaps. Beyond the hills.

So much easier to keep it on that level.

"They're like us really aren't they?" said Sarah.

"Who are?" I asked.

"The Yugoslavs," Sarah said, "they're like the generations of our family. Staying together, splitting up, nothing seems to be right."

Mum and I glanced at each other, neither of us was up to answering that at present. If, indeed, there was an answer to it.

"Perhaps yours will be the generation to get it right, Sarah," I said, "let's hope so anyway, you're our future."

Then Mum said, "Hey, aren't we going to drink a toast to Iain before we finish all his whisky?"

"There's another bottle in the sideboard," said Sarah.

Mum topped up our glasses, "This'll be more than enough, young lady, thank you."

Sarah turned to me, "Mum, are you going to say it in Serbo-Croat? Gran and I won't understand the words, but we'll know what you mean, and it's sort of the language he lived in, at the end, isn't it?"

Mum put her glass down on the carpet.

"You think she should do it in Gàidhlig?" Sarah asked her.

Mum sighed, "Sure, language is just a means of communication," she said.

"Thinking that, Mother," I said, "is why you're a painter."

"Funny," she said, "I thought it was for the talent I have – and all the work I've put into its development."

"Don't you wish you'd started sooner?" asked Sarah, "taken your painting further."

Approaching footsteps on the street outside.

I turned off the gaz, told them to be quiet.

Just a couple, talking about her mother who was ill.

Mum handed the matches to Sarah, and she relit the gaz. Neither of them said anything. I could feel the sweat cooling on my face.

Then, "No, love," said Mum, "I'm glad I can paint – for itself, and for the passport to all it's been in my life, but I have no illusions, it's just a small talent I have, and this way I'll not outlive it. Terrible that must be, when it happens."

She smiled at Sarah, picked up her glass again. "That's not likely to happen to you. Roberto's not as biased as me, and he thinks you can really make something of it."

"If that's what you want for yourself, love," I said.

"Yes, Mum, it is," said Sarah.

Mum raised her glass, "To new beginnings," she said.

And we raised our glasses to hers.

Then I asked Mum to toast Dad for us. And she did.

Twenty Two

It came as a shock when they gave me a date to begin my gradual leaving of the hospital. I'd thought I was ready to leave, to begin to make a life for myself again, but I wasn't. How could I be without knowing what had happened to Sarah?

Alasdair it was came to take me to the house for my first weekend at 'home'. The first time I'd been back in it since.

It was difficult to get out of the car but, for once, he just let me take my time. I needn't have worried, the woman from the agency had been there before us – dusted and polished with a spray, and an enthusiasm, that were alien to me. The vases too she'd filled with laburnum. So it didn't smell like home.

"Come and see you've got everything you need," he said. I followed him towards the dining room. They'd moved everything down and made it into a bedroom for me.

By the time I got there he'd got my few things unpacked and mostly into the drawers already.

"Aye," I said, after a cursory look round. "That's fine Alasdair, and the perfect place too for feeling appropriate if I want a midnight feast in my bed."

He put my nightdress on the bed, I saw the hands of him lingering on its shoulder.

"Virginia going with you to Glasgow, is she?" I asked.

"No," he said reddening, but at least he had the grace not to pretend.

"No," he said, "that was a mistake. We didn't bring out the best in each other. I didn't know you knew."

He looked at me as if he expected me to be able to think of something suitable to say.

I just wanted him to go.

And clearly he did himself for almost immediately he started back again to the lounge. I had to sit down on the bed for a few minutes till I could haul myself up onto my zimmer frame again and follow him.

When I got there he was standing looking out of the window at the garden which was patchy with overgrowth and dark bare wounds where recently someone had started to get to grips with it.

He came across and took my arm and helped me into the chair. He was still wearing the same aftershave he'd always worn.

"Well," he said, "that's you."

"Alasdair," I said, "I think I should go back. Go back to Roberto's. We started from there, if I went – retraced our steps, so to speak – then perhaps it'd all come back to me. What happened."

He went and sat in the chair opposite me. Crossed his legs. He was smiling a wry smile.

"You're meaning," he said, "that if you had organising all that, doing all that, to think about, you hope you might be able to halt the memories that are coming to you now too thick and fast."

The silence between us grew.

"I don't blame you," he said at last, and his voice was almost gentle.

I looked up and saw there was a gentleness in his smile too, that had reached even, a little, to his eyes. I felt my own eyes filling with tears and looked away.

"Kate," he said, and then we were holding each other, and he was crying too.

✦

But there were no more dreams then for a couple of weeks – just the gruelling struggle to get some life back into my body, to force myself to make arrangements for a future I couldn't yet see.

So it seemed a relief when Hartmutt suggested we go out for the day. Like escaping for a while.

It was cold at Hadrian's Wall, the wind was whipping across the hills. So it reminded me of home. And that was no escape at all.

I could feel Hartmutt standing behind me, sheltering me, but I could see only the hills and the sky.

"Hartmutt," I said, then, in the Gàidhlig, knowing he wouldn't be able to understand my words, I said, "I've led her to something terrible, left her. How can I ever live with that?"

He was still for a while, then he come round to my side and bent down and round to me in my chair till our eyes were on the level.

"Kate," he said, then, in the German, "you know that I love you." He stood again, paused, asked, "Do you want to talk about it?"

"No," I said, "not now."

"Alright," he said, "I will go for a walk on the Wall." He waved his arm towards it, "I'll be down-wind of you, just shout if you want anything."

He waited for a minute just in case, I suppose, I would say anything more. He then bent and kissed me on the cheek.

"Oh, look," I said, and his eyes followed the pointing of my finger to where a lamb was bouncing as if on springs, four feet together, as they do – you know.

"Ah," he said grinning, "the Spring. Hope springs eternal . . . I'd better walk quietly so as not to disturb his parents at their courting."

"Hartmutt man," I said, "how can you have got to your age without knowing? Sheep only have sex in November."

He stood and half-turned from me, "It may surprise you to know," he said, "that great tracts of my life haven't been spent contemplating the sex lives of sheep."

"Sorry," I said, though I wasn't just sure why he was so angry.

"You're so much a part of my life," I said, "that I forget, sometimes, that our heritages are so different."

"Kate, heritage is the rocks of foundation from which we build not the capstones of our graves."

He bent and kissed me again, not so gently. "I'll just go and get you another rug from the car," he said. Then he turned and left me.

✦

I could feel the air shimmering in the spaces where the sounds had been. I became aware of something rough under my cheek. I opened my eyes, turned my head slightly. Carpet. There were arms wound around my thighs from behind, the fingers digging in, a face pressed against my calves. I could feel the hot, jagged breathing. I raised myself on an elbow and twisted round to look. Mum. She was quivering.

Beyond her the water that the chrysanthemums had stood in too long was still spreading scum surfaced over the faded green of the carpet, it's dank smell rising tinged metal-edged with blood. I struggled to get my legs free. The sound of breathing was very loud. She wouldn't let go. I struggled harder. My foot thudded into something soft and she let out a gasping cry, but loosened her grip just enough for me to get away.

I tried to stand, but my feet just seemed to wobble around. I crawled over to Sarah's makeshift bed. I pulled the duvet up to cover the soft impression that'd been left by her lying on the mattress. It was still warm.

I picked up her pyjamas. The buttons bit cold and hard into my hand.

✦

I looked down at my palms. There were red semi-circles where I'd dug my nails in. They were sore. The wind caught my hair and whipped it across my face. I turned my face up and into the wind and my hair streamed out behind me. It felt fresh and clean, and for a moment I thought of taking the brakes off the wheelchair and hurtling down hill, feeling the wind washing right through me. Maybe I'd crash, maybe I'd fly, but at least I'd be moving.

But I just sat and watched the clouds racing, shape-changing, across the sky.

Then Hartmutt returned.

He knelt by my chair so our heads would be at the same level. He tucked the rug in then picked up my hand. I could feel the warmth of him.

"Kate," he said, "Darling, I think we've all gradually come to accept that she's dead."

Into the lengthening silence he quietly said, "Is that what you were trying to tell me before?"

I managed to nod my head, it didn't go in quite the right direction, but it was easier than speaking.

He stroked my hand for a while.

"Kate," he said, "can't you tell me?"

I tried to shake my head, but it wouldn't go.

"I don't know," I said. "I don't know what happened, just, somehow, I know she's . . ."

"That she's dead," he finished for me.

"I could be wrong, couldn't I?"

He kissed my hand. We were both silent.

"It's not very likely you're wrong," he said at last.

He knelt where he was for a time, and we neither of us spoke. The wind whistled around us, across the hills.

"When Marie died," he said, "I felt so guilty."

I could feel his hand tightening on mine.

"I loved her, knew how much I'd miss her. And I did want her suffering to end. For her own sake. But I wanted my own having to watch her to end too. I felt, sometimes, after, as if that thought had killed her. As if my having survived that ordeal, when she hadn't, was wrong – my fault. I thought I was the only person who'd ever felt anything like that. Now I know most people do. Something like that.

"You seemed to understand that, then.

"Kate, Sarah chose to go to Trieste, from what you say she initiated it. She was young, but she wasn't a child. Don't blame yourself."

I looked beyond him to the Wall. To the clouds racing, shape-changing, across the back-lit grey-blue of the sky. To the lovely gentle curves of the hills, and the Wall marching across them in a straight line. Keeping out the good as well as the bad.

One thing most of us are good at, aren't we? building walls.

And I couldn't think of anything to say.

Eventually he got to his feet again, a little stiffly.

Then I watched as the familiar solidity of him went down the dip into the shelter hidden from my sight and out again climbing onto the top opposite, where he strode along leaning into the wind. The sky was bright, it hurt my eyes.

Twenty Three

I lay for a while with my mother's arm flung across my shoulder. She was snoring. On her mattress on the floor Sarah was curled up, her hair streaming red gold over the pillow. So young.

◆

Roberto waved goodbye to us from the street door. His feet were still bare.

We got on the train with mixed feelings, but, I think, it wasn't until we reached the UNPROFOR post at Trieste and met the others that the actuality of the situation began to impinge. I'd translated at many meetings in trouble zones – but only for the leaders, always before I'd been insulated from the reality of the people.

Then, beyond the camp, I lost all feeling of reality.

We parked our lorry, it was empty in minutes. And ourselves silent.

Children fighting for morsels of luxury when they lacked the most basic necessity. Gifts for the donor, not the recipient.

Buildings – people – derelict, broken.

Images familiar, but now not transient. And there're no smells on the television, no cold, none of the atmosphere that there is here of unbearable feelings intensified until they crystallise out leaving only blankness.

All I can see are their eyes.

I'm here because I'm supposed to know the language. How can I interpret when I can't even begin to understand?

◆

They dropped us off back in Trieste, we stayed overnight, washed our clothes, pretended to sleep.

We got on the train for Hungary that passed through Zagreb. We rattled on into the night with the both of them sleeping. One of my talents – sleeping – it seemed to have eluded me for now, though the heavy image-battered wooziness of me was so wanting it to come.

And I kept hearing the noises, the sudden noises. Myself jumping, cringing inside. Shaking. Not coping as well as the others. And I know I've inherited a sensitivity, a weakness, from Dad.

And, try as I might not to, I kept remembering, that as I gave out my Christmas shoe boxes of goodies – despite all I could see and feel around me, despite what I knew had gone on, was going on, would go on around me – the comfort I was wanting was for myself.

They say you get deadened to it all after a while – for survival. But we are all deadened, and what is it that survives that? And for what?

Twenty Four

Hartmutt reappeared over the brow of the hill opposite and I watched as he walked through the long grass down. He was moving much more freely now, striding along. He looked up towards me and waved before he was lost to my sight in the dip and during the climb back up again to me.

And I'm thinking now of the other people in Trieste. Those, too few to be sure, I'd seen but not recognised at the time. People who'd persisted and survived. More than intact. People we couldn't pity, or despise.

And perhaps I am beginning to understand a little at last. Not the alphabet of others. But ours.

Hartmutt arrived, ruddy faced and slightly out of breath at my side. But relaxed, the walk had done him good.

"Hartmutt," I said, "do you remember that time in Italy? You know at Domenico's monastery."

"Yes," he said.

"Well, you knew didn't you? Knew even before we got there that I couldn't leave Alasdair because of Sarah, because of how my own childhood had been? How I couldn't let hers become."

"Yes" he said, "Yes, I suppose I did. And it is, always was, a decision the intention of which I can't help but respect." He put his hands into the pockets of his cords, and looked up to the skyline, "but between knowing and being told there's a lot of room for hope."

"Hartmutt," I said.

He turned back towards me, "Yes, what is it?" He seemed a little distracted.

"You know when we go back?" I asked.

He nodded.

"Well," I said, "would it be alright, do you mind if we go back to your flat – not to the house."

"Of course, love," he said, "No problem."

"Will we have to buy anything to eat?" I asked.

"Don't think so," he said, "I've got quite a bit in. Hungry are you?"

"Parts of me are starving," I said.

He put his hand on my shoulder, and after a long pause he said, "I could make us some goulash, if you fancy that. My speciality."

"Actually I was thinking more of courgette flower fritters."

He frowned for a moment, then grinned, "Yes," he said, "I remember, they were quite sweet, weren't they – then the bitterness of the pollen on their stamens."

He smiled at me, "I'm pretty sure there's some saffron in the cupboard, I could put that into the dumplings," he said.

We returned along the coast road. The sea was wild with the wind. Neither of us seemed to have anything to say.

Back in his flat he helped me into my chair by the window. In his touch I became aware of my own coldness. He turned the central heating down a little and lit the fire and we sat in silence for a while watching the flames take hold. A blue tinge they had to the yellow of them – from the frost.

After a while he sighed and got to his feet, "Better get this meal started," he said, "the meat will take a while to cook."

He headed for the kitchen and I heard him opening and closing cupboard doors, muttering to himself under his breath. He came back and put his head round the corner of the kitchen door.

"Can't find the saffron," he said, "how about turmeric?"

"Aye," I smiled at him, "that'll do just fine."

After a while sitting watching the flames roaring with the wind up the chimney I stood, and, hanging on to what I could, I made my way over to the pile of records on the shelf behind the old record player. I searched till I found the record by the Rolling Stones, then subsided thankfully to the floor. I put the record on the player, found the track 'Ruby Tuesday.'

The quiet beginning took me by surprise, I'd always thought of the Stones as raucous somehow. Energetic. Hartmutt and Alasdair must have forgotten that bit too.

I settled to listen to the words none of us now knew, but then I heard, 'Goodbye . . .', and my mind just seemed to drift off and I found I'd got to the end without listening to the rest of the words, so, as on another occasion, with another record, I put it back to the beginning and played it again.

But it was no use, my mind just didn't want to listen, and all I heard over and over again were the last flutey notes fading into the air. And, somehow, I no longer knew why it'd seemed so important to remember the words.

All that time ago.

So, I took the record off the deck, and put it back into its tattered sleeve. I glanced up at the book-shelf, but it seemed too far now above my head and I just slipped the record under the carpet where it was loose by the wall under the shelves.

I hauled myself to my feet and, despite the uncontrollable wobbling of my knees, I got myself back to my chair, flopped down into it. I was head-ringingly out of breath but I could feel myself grinning.

I looked out of the window at the sea. The waves were crashing against the pier, sending great jets of spray spurting high into the air. The lighthouse at the end of the pier was just beginning to light up, though the sky was still a clear blue with the clouds fleeing across it before the wind. You could almost feel the energy of it.

They were right. I should trust my mind – it was telling me something. Telling me there was no point in trying to remember at all.

Twenty Five

"What is it, love?" I asked.

"They're all crumpled," she said. There were tears in her eyes.

"Oh, Sarah," I said, "they're the most beautiful present I've ever had."

◆

But it's not the vast expanse of leg I'm looking at, it's my hand in Dad's.

◆

And the sun is warm to the top of my head. The sea is cold to my feet. The sea gulls call, and the wind soughs in the sea-ward slant of the blossom-laden trees and petals scatter with their fragrance on the air, float on the salt tang of the waves.

Pink.

There's tea around the fire, with the flames leaping red and gold crackling up the black crust sculpture of the chimney.

Warm.

◆

The kitchen Sarah's never known.

◆

They'd found a bottle of whisky in his flat and on our return there we sat, red of nose and ear, round the camping gaz, with his chunky Bohemian red and gold wine glasses, well filled, slippily clutched in our gloves.

Mum took a sip of her drink. "If he'd been just a few months younger he'd have missed the War completely. Life can change in a moment."

"Yes, Mum," I said, "but it can change for the better too."

I caught Sarah smiling at me, far too cynically for someone of her age. "I wish you could have known us, Sarah," I said, "when first we were married. Your Dad and me."

How wonderfully familiar he'd seemed, amongst the strangeness of the city. But that time'd been so good too – the freedom of the anonymity of it, that only someone else brought up so claustrophobically could appreciate. Life opening out.

But we failed to move on, we had suffocated – something. I suppose some of us carry our islands with us.

"I'm sorry, love," I said, "we didn't give you as good a start as we might have – as we wanted."

"How can you know that?" asked Sarah. "If you didn't know where I was going, how could you know where the right place to start was?"

There was a movement outside, and we all turned to look, myself half standing. But it was just some litter blowing against the fence. The wind was getting up.

"You don't have just the one start anyway," said Mum, "it's again, and again, and again."

"Yes, I know," I said, "I am going to do something about it, Mum. Perhaps us all coming here is the start of it. Sarah's alright now."

"Thank God for that," said Sarah, "I felt it was my fault sometimes – when I was younger, I mean – that you weren't happy, that it was all my fault making you stay together when you both might have been better alone, or with someone else. Sometimes I was just glad you were both there for me."

"And," said Mum, raising her glass to me, "there's always your whirlwind romance with Hartmutt."

"I've got to get my life sorted out first, Mum," I said, "I have let it drift into a sort of limbo, I suppose."

Then we all drifted into a silence of our own thoughts, into a silence of avoiding thoughts, until Sarah suddenly said, "It's him as well, isn't it?"

"Who?" Mum asked.

Sarah took another sip of her whisky. "Hartmutt. It's like," she paused. "You know, in the Gulf War? That tower – minaret sort of thing – they showed it over and over again in slow motion on the telly. That tower they computer bombed. And what's-his-name, the newsreader, said all portentously that we'd entered an era of clean, impersonal war."

She straightened her legs and leant back against the wall. She had great dark patches under her eyes.

"That was when they made up 'collateral damage' wasn't it?" Sarah said. "And that's what we all are, isn't it? Grandad and Hartmutt from the Second World War, and Gran and Mum and Dad and me – it's sort of like as if the bomb on the tower was a stone in a loch and the ripples keep going on out and out making more people collateral. Damaged, I mean. And there's more towers now than there ever have been in the world before. And our's is a tiny stone, and we're far out ripples compared to these people, these last few days."

She took another great gulp of whisky. "I don't want to – I can't think of them till home." She pushed her hair back with her glove. "I want to think of something else." Her voice trailed off, close to tears.

"Well," said Mum, "at least, with your family background, Sarah, you won't ruin your life reaching for unattainable perfection."

"Aye," I said, "at least there's that."

Twenty Six

Hartmutt come in from the kitchen.

"The meat's on," he said, "but turmeric won't do. Let's do things properly."

So we decided he'd go to the shops for his saffron and some wine after dropping me off at St Mary's, to see Mum, and to deliver the paint she'd asked for. Blue for her sky.

When we got to the hospital they showed us to her room – she'd never allowed us to see her there before.

A bowed window she had, on the second floor, overlooking the misted glass of the conservatory roof. Through it you could see the vague shapes and colours of the plants. Like an impressionistic painting it was.

She was standing when Hartmutt wheeled me in, just finishing turning her easel so the picture she was painting was facing the wall. She was wearing her painting shirt.

Propped against the wall was the drying picture of the mountains and the mist – and the sea in the background. The view from her studio window at home.

When he'd gone we sat looking at one another for a while, then she stood and turned her easel round to me so I could see. She was painting a portrait of Sarah. Head and shoulders just, with her hair lifting as if in the wind.

"I wish Roberto had painted her – instead of me again," she said.

"Mum, you know what's happened, don't you?" I asked.

"No," she said.

I walked over to the window and looked out to the garden. The old man was there with his hand cupped around his cigarette. I could see the smoke rising from between his fingers. Grey and curling dispersing on the breeze. I could smell it.

There was smoke, choking wreaths of black smoke. Desert, oil rigs. I was wandering alone bare foot. The sand was burning my feet. I could smell them. Even through the smoke I could smell them.

Faces of the men they had taken, the bailed out pilot and the navigator. Beaten. The faces of the men. Sarah's face. Faces rushing towards me through the smoke, disappearing just before I thought they must hit me.

The tower, the tower computer bombed. And the newsreader's smug voice-over telling us we'd entered the era of clean, impersonal war.

Hartmutt came then and took me back to the flat. I opened the car window to clear the smell of the smoke. Cold it was.

Twenty Seven

But when we got back to his flat it was filled with the smell of the goulash. And with warmth. Hartmutt helped me into my chair by the window and went with his shopping into the kitchen.

I started saying my multiplication tables, but I couldn't get my mind to stay in the present.

✦

It was approaching midnight when we reached the station. Ive was there to pick us up as arranged. Now I knew what I'd been asking to get him to meet us there. I tried to tell him that − that I hadn't known − he just brushed it aside. But he was angry with us. I could feel it. He said he'd done it for the memory of Dad, not for us.

He drove us through the wide boulevards of Zagreb. I don't know where he'd managed to get the petrol. We drove past St. Stephen's Cathedral − difficult to miss it − and from there on out to Dad's flat.

Ive just dropped us off, he wouldn't come in with us. He said he was going to stay with his wife's people, up in the hills, for Christmas. We didn't give him the presents we'd bought him. They'd seemed appropriate when we'd left.

Dad's flat was just as it always had been. Only dusty, cobwebby and cold. It was difficult to really believe neither Mum nor Sarah had ever been there.

Ive came round next morning to make sure we were alright before leaving for the hills − he said he was staying up there until Spring. He was still angry with us for coming. Told us we should leave as soon as possible, it wasn't safe. In the clearer light of morning he looked old, and strained, and tired.

"But it's peaceful now," I protested. "Up here anyway."

"Just because your Western reporters aren't here recording what's happening, doesn't mean nothing is," he said. "You don't know what our reality is. Maybe we don't want anyone to know what it is. Though soon they will all forget – think it's all over, but for most of us it probably will never be over. At least your father understood that. Isn't it bad enough without all the superficial voyeurs?"

"We came to say goodbye to Dad, to sort things out," I protested. That had seemed such a good reason, so important, in Britain. I didn't mention the parcels.

"I meant the reporters," he said, but I knew he wasn't telling the truth.

He just turned then and left, no longer the man I once knew. I stood watching him till Sarah came and touched my arm, "What did he say, Mum?" she asked.

"He misses your Granddad," I told her.

✦

"Sometimes I felt it was my fault," said Sarah, "that you had to stay together and be unhappy because of me. Sometimes I was just glad you were both there."

✦

"No, Sarah," I said, "I feel the best part of my life is just beginning, I can begin to think, now, what I want for myself, I have some idea at last what that might be.

✦

"Sarah," I said, "come away from that window."

And in the distance was the rumble of thunder. In the distance there was the rumble we could no longer convince ourselves was thunder.

Then there was the sound of heavy running footsteps, coming closer. Voices low growling. Gunshots, very close. Snipers.

Then there was the silhouette of a man, I could see him – through the window, standing against the light.

Sarah.

Heavy running footsteps. Receding.

Smoke. Wreaths.

✦

I woke with a start. The moonlight came filtered palely glittering through the thick frost patterns between the curtains where we hadn't pulled them properly across. But all was quiet. Just the sounds of Mum's ragged breathing.

I needed to go to the bathroom. I looked towards the door. It was closed. I watched the door handle. It didn't seem to be moving. I managed to get my legs over the edge of the bed. Holding the table I levered myself up into an almost standing position. Bent over like an old crone I hobbled to the door. I stood holding the door handle listening to my breathing. To the uneven thudding of my heart. I opened the door.

He was there again.

I closed the door and leant against it, a mist I knew wasn't there rising towards me from the floor.

I had to go out. I had to go out. The only alternative was to stay in this room for ever.

He was round the corner. At ninety degrees to me. His side toward me. His back to the wall. There was room to get past.

I opened the door. He was still there. His dark cloak hooded over the shape of him.

I fast-limped past him and slammed the bathroom door locking it shut behind me. I leant against it, my breath coming in sobs.

Later I knew I would have to go back.

When I opened the bathroom door he was still there. Beyond the bedroom, with his side to it. Facing me now. The long hood drooping forward. His head bent. His arms folded, their hands up the opposite sleeves. His dark cloak hooded over the shape of him.

I couldn't run. Slowly I walked towards him. Towards the door of the bedroom. Keeping an eye on him. Keeping a hand on the wall.

I saw his head beginning to move just as I began to get close to the door. I stopped. I stood and watched as he lifted his head. He lifted his head and looked full at me.

Looked at me with his eyes black holes of seeing in the skull that was all of his face.

The same it was. Night after night after night.

Till, one night, I knew I no longer had the strength to walk over to the door, to open it hoping he wouldn't be there. Fearing he would do something.

I don't know where the idea to leave the door open came from. But in the end that's what I did.

He moved gradually round, so as we slept he stood filling the doorway watching us. Unmoving.

Eventually the night came when fear was just a part of being. So, when I needed to get up, I got up.

I walked towards him. I looked him full in the face. And he turned till he was at ninety degrees to me. His side towards me. The dank cold of his cloak brushed me as I passed.

But he never came again after that.

Twenty Eight

Hartmutt came back in with a glass of wine for me.

He put it on the table beside me. A deep red the wine was, with the colours of the fire in it. Hartmutt kissed me, then reminded me that Alasdair was due to be dropping by later at the house with some papers for me to sign – asked me if I wanted to cancel, or tell him where we were.

"No," I said, "don't cancel. It should only take a couple of minutes and he's off to Glasgow in the morning with Alan, to sort out a lab for their new project. Let's get everything finished, out of the way. Then we can have our meal in peace."

He picked up the mobile phone and started for the kitchen, "I'll make the dumplings when I've phoned him," he said, "it shouldn't take too long."

◆

I can feel the air shimmering in the spaces where the sounds had been.

Something rough under my cheek. Carpet. Arms are wound around my thighs, fingers digging in. I feel the hot, jagged breathing. I twist round to look. Mum. Quivering.

Beyond her the water that the chrysanthemums have stood in too long is spreading scum surfaced over the faded green of the carpet. The dank smell rises tinged metal-edged with blood. I struggle to get my legs free. The sound of breathing is very loud. She won't let go. I struggle harder. My foot thuds into something soft and she lets out a gasping cry, and loosenes her grip just enough for me to get free.

I try to stand, but my feet just seem to wobble around. I crawl over to Sarah's bed. I pull the duvet up to cover the soft impression of her body in the mattress. It's still warm.

I pick up her pyjamas. The buttons bite cold and hard into my hand.

It's dark. I'm sitting on the floor by the window. I move to ease the pain in my legs, but the tape across the starburst in the pane is almost opaque, and I move slightly to the left to avoid it.

The breath-cleared patch in the multi-layered ice patterns is already feathering over, and I breathe on it again, rub at its grittiness with my sleeve. There's maybe a lightening in the sky to the East. It reflects off the ice-patches in the trodden snow.

Somewhere behind me I can hear my mother. She's still breathing.

I wake with a start. Moonlight through the curtains. Quiet. Just Mum's ragged breathing. I look towards her. She's still sitting close to the wall, knees up – wrapped in the blankets, gently rocking. Still sucking her thumb. I don't speak to her, I can no longer bear her not answering.

I look to the door.

He's there again.

A mist I know isn't there is rising towards me from off the floor.

His eyes black holes of seeing in the skull that is all of his face.

Again and again. Every night the same.

The night came when fear was just a part of being. So, when I needed to get up, I got up. The dank cold of his cloak brushed me as I passed.

But he never came again after that.

I went into the living room. Sarah was lying on the floor. I went and touched her. She was cold. I tried to lift her shoulders but the dried blood was sticking her skin to the carpet, and her skin just stretched and wouldn't let me turn her over. I had to tear her free. I struggled to get the pyjama jacket on her. She was all floppy and wouldn't help. I managed to hoist her up onto the futon. Covered her with the duvet. That would warm her up. I picked the chrysanthemums from off the floor. Some of the petals fell from them, but there was nothing else. I gave them to her to hold.

I picked up the fallen petals, took them out to the bin. The cold seemed to have got right into me. I could hardly bend to the bin. As if the cold were freezing my body into one piece.

When I went back into the flat I smelled the smell of it. Of Mum and myself. I gathered snow, and melted it on the camping gaz. Had a wash and changed. Washed and changed Mother, she didn't protest. Her eyes were glazed. We'd been still wearing the clothes we'd had on when we'd arrived. I didn't know now when that was. I put the old clothes in the bin.

I left the gaz on, by the futon – she'd be cold. Then I got Mum and myself out. Just took her hand and she came with me. Everything seemed sort of frozen somehow, but my mind was very clear. I pulled the door shut behind us. I had that feeling, you know, as if I'd forgotten something. But I couldn't just think what it was.

At the corner I turned and looked back. There was smoke, thin wreaths of black smoke. I could smell them. Someone must have found something, somewhere, to burn.

I felt a bit strange. Everything seemed slowed down, sort of rippling. As if I was walking through water.

There was black smoke. Swirling. Swirling in wreaths. There was fire behind us.

Explosion.

Dad's flat. Explosion.

Debris falling. Falling in slow motion around us. Thudding into us, my arms, my back. Her head bleeding. Falling, crawling, keeping on.

Pain in my back.

Pain.

✦

We slept that night in Ive's flat, the lock on the door was already broken. I don't know how long we stayed, we stayed until we were stronger. Then it took us nearly half a day to get to the station. My back was alright as long as I didn't try to bend. She just held my hand. We got on the first train that was going in roughly the right direction. I just wanted to get out.

When we got to the Istrian peninsula things seemed more as they should be. We stopped for a while, sat and watched as the sun set, white and misted like a full moon, into the white-flecked darkness of the sea.

An old man helped me down onto the deck. I didn't think I was going to be able to make it.

He gave my arm a tug and I landed heavily. We hauled Mum aboard just as they cast off.

We lowered ourselves to the wet deck close to the pole in its centre. We sailed from the harbour straight into the wind. We clung to each other.

Cold the sea looked. Rough.

The boat yawed and creaked and my mind blanked into the rhythm of it.

When first we saw land it was difficult to believe it was real, though there were seagulls in plenty wheeling and crying to tell us it was so. I had to struggle to try to remember where it might be.

Then I saw the tall thin Barbers poles on the jetties.

They helped us ashore.

Mum and I just stood for a while, as people scurried away. Soon there were just the two of us. I couldn't think what it was we were supposed to do.

Mum was shivering and shuddering so I started to walk, pulling her along roughly till she got going. Walking. Walking.

Then we got to a square that looked familiar.

We stood for a while. Then I noticed we were shaking. I suppose it must have been cold. We started to move again, first in one direction, then in another. And we're staggering a bit now. My head swimming.

'Come on,' I told myself, 'you've got to get us there.' I still wasn't sure where it was we were going, but, somehow, I knew I'd recognise it when we got there.

Arches. Bridges. The slap and stench of water. Footfalls echoing. Then, suddenly, a building I knew.

I kept my finger on the bell till one of the shutters was angrily thrust open.

Then, there was the soft padding of feet on the stair. And the door opening.

Garlic and turpentine.

Roberto.

✦

I lay for a while with my mother's arm flung across my shoulder. She was snoring quite loudly. I turned my head and looked over the edge of the bed. Dingy red carpet.

I carefully eased my mother's arm from round me and managed to get my feet to the floor. She stirred and gave a little groan, but she didn't wake.

I made my way across the studio towards the bathroom, my hand against the wall. In the early morning light the canvases cast monstrous shadows against the walls.

I heard the padding of feet, and turning saw Roberto coming towards me, barefoot, bare-legged in a blue and white striped nightshirt. He looked tense and old. He put his arm around my shoulders, helped me to the toilet, back towards bed. My feet started to wobble around and I staggered with him crashing into an easel. There was a stabbing pain in my back. My legs didn't want to stand. Somehow he helped me into bed.

I felt cold. Woozy. Floaty. But there's no pain. There's a strange nothingness of no pain.

He stood for a while, I could see him through a thickening mist, looking at Mum and at me. He had tears in his eyes. On his cheeks.

✦

So, there's the dingy pastel pink of the ceiling, and the wall at the bottom of the bed, and the clock with its second hand jerking round the yellow of its face. In the distance I could hear the rattle of the drinks trolley, voices, the TV. I knew the window was to the side of me, where I could see out if only I could turn my head.

✦

"Sarah," I said, "come away from that window."

✦

The sea gulls call, and the wind soughs in the sea-ward slant of the blossom-laden trees and petals scatter with their fragrance on the air, float on the salt tang of the waves.

Pink.

There's tea around the fire, with the flames leaping red and gold crackling up the black crust sculpture of the chimney.

✦

And that's where we should be now, and Alasdair with us, in that kitchen that Sarah's never known.

That we never made.

✦

"Mum," said Sarah, "you're useless – fancy being frightened of thunder at your age." She was grinning, glad to be one up on me, but I could see her fear too – in her eyes.

"Sarah," I said, "come away from that window."

✦

Beyond her the water that the chrysanthemums had stood in too long was still spreading, scum surfaced, over the faded green of the carpet, it's dank smell rising tinged metal-edged with blood. The sound of breathing was very loud.

✦

"Mum," said Sarah, "you're useless – fancy being frightened of thunder at your age." She was grinning, glad to be one up on me, but I could see her fear too – in her eyes.

"Sarah," I said, "come away from that window."

"Sarah."

And in the distance was the rumble of thunder. In the hills in the distance the rumble we knew wasn't thunder. Flashes of light and cracks of sound. Fighting in the hills. Then there were heavy running footsteps in the street outside. And voices low growling.

Snipers. Panic. Screaming.

◆

"Sarah," I said, "come away from that window." And through the window in the street beyond her I could see the silhouette of a man. Blotting out the light. Saying something to someone else. Other people in the street outside. A roaring in my ears.

One shot.

Heavy running footsteps. Receding. The water from the can he'd dropped gurgling down into the gutter.

Blood and lumps dripping down inside the window, from the ceiling.

The flop of her body to the floor.

Her eyes.

Her eyes.

Her eyes open and sightless.

The thud of Dad's gun on the floor.

My still opening hand tingling from its firing.

Twenty Nine

I could hear singing.

A man was singing Brahms' Lullaby in German. In German and in hums where he didn't know the words.

Hartmutt.

I could smell the warm smells of cooking.

The front door-bell rang and I heard Hartmutt swear, then he came into the room, and crossed it to press the entry intercom button. On the screen beyond him I could see the hazy image of a man. In one movement Hartmutt pressed the door release button and turned to look at me.

He was still standing, as if frozen, looking at me, his finger on the release button when Alasdair came into the room.

Alasdair came in fast and was half-way across the room before he glanced at Hartmutt. Then Alasdair stopped where he was and turned to look back at me.

Under his arm were some papers and in his hand was a plant in a blue and white ceramic pot.

A pot chrysanthemum. Small the flowers of it were.

Pink.

I heard a cry behind me and turned to look, my eyes unfocussed, out of the window at the surging sea and a seagull crying a fluttering smudge against the blue of the sky.

I felt the rising panic, but reached for the mantelpiece and used it to pull myself up.

I stood and turned.

And in the unbearable silence liquefying around me I took a step towards them into the reality which had become mine.